Stand Tall, Harry

by Mary Mahony

Illustrated by Catherine M. Larkin

Always stand tall.

Mary Mahony

Redding Press • Belmont, MA

Susan A. Pasternack, Editor

Illustrations © Catherine M. Larkin

Cover and interior design © TLC Graphics, www.tlcgraphics.com

Printed by Bang Printing, Brainerd, MN

Portrait on page 133 © Joe Demb Photography, 59 Louise Rd., Belmont, MA 02478

Fiction

RL: 4

Library of Congress Control Number: 2001119810

ISBN 0-9658879-2-8

A Lesson For The Adults Who Guide Our Young Readers

I grew up in Redding, Connecticut, which was a very White suburban community in the 1960s. When I was in high school, a family way ahead of the rest of the world brought an African-American student, Lloyd Harrington, from Alabama to Connecticut to give him a chance for a "better" education. It has taken me almost fifty years to appreciate what a difficult time that must have been for Lloyd. He must have missed his family and culture more than any of us ever appreciated. I often wonder if the experience was really "better" or if it was just our own misperception of a culture we never understood because we never took the time or were never encouraged to do so.

I graduated from high school in 1966, and that very same year, almost 200 miles away, the METCO program was being started in Boston. The METCO program is an interdistrict voluntary school desegregation effort. Today, after more than thirty-five years, it is the oldest program of this type still in operation. What began as 320 African-American students being bused to outlying suburban schools, now consists of some 3,100 youngsters and is still growing. Although it gives opportunities to many students, it also has it drawbacks, to which many White communities have closed their minds and their eyes. For a person from any minority cultural background in a community school that is mostly White, the experience is not always the smooth journey that the idealists extol. It is a journey that provides moments of loneliness and sadness as well as feelings of not measuring up to the expectations of communities whose standards are sometimes almost too high. It's hard to reach for the stars when they keep moving higher in the sky.

One of the things that many students have noted to me over the years is the lack of diversity among staff people. Clearly, however, to the credit of those students who are bused to these communities, in time they become more comfortable and accept their new environment, often keeping their opinions to themselves. Their ability to make the transition and adjust is something to be admired and I often stand in awe of my own students as I watch them adapt.

Another group mentioned only rarely are the minority students who live in these White communities. I recall an incident involving a Black student and a crossing guard who assumed the student she was helping lived in Boston and was visiting the White friend standing next to her. As the story goes, the crossing guard made small talk with the Black student, thinking she was staying in town to visit her local friend that day. To be fair, I think the woman was trying to make conversation and be friendly, but her presumption was inexcusable. Actually, this young Black girl lived in a very nice house not too far from that corner. Experiences such as this one indicate a mind-set that is still very much a part of our country and our world. And imagine how this very poised young woman must have felt.

This way of thinking also suggests that Boston students don't live in homes that are as special as those in these outlying communities. Not true at all, and, in fact, it is quite pricey to live in Boston and its urban "burbs." We all have a long way to go, myself included.

In 1998, thanks to a forward-thinking vision, teachers in my own school system were offered the opportunity to take a course called "Empowering Multicultural Initiatives." Carroll Blake and Elli Stern, who taught my particular section, have a place in both my heart and my mind somewhere near God. It is my hope that the time will come in our society when courses like this no longer need to be taught and books will no longer be written about White privilege and the racism and prejudice that exists in us all. We will then finally have a world in which we all live together as one. It is very clear to me, however, that I may not be around to see this dream come true.

Stand Tall, Harry is a book that blends both the social and medical worlds and teaches us lessons on life that will live on in each one of us as we all learn to "stand tall" and together be proud of who we are. Perhaps Grampy and Harry will help all of us to open our minds and our hearts to continue to build a better world.

Dedication

This book is dedicated to Thelma Burns, Carroll Blake, and Elli Stern, and to those students who have shared with me things about life that are not always found in books. Each one of these people will continue to "stand tall" in my mind and in my heart for their generous support and sharing. I hope we all will continue to work toward empowering multicultural initiatives, not only in the Boston area, but throughout the world.

A special thanks to:

Marc, Asher, M.D.	Carroll Blake
Nan Braucher	Thelma Burns
Tom Colburn, C.O.	Linda Ferguson
Allison Guillory	Lloyd Harrington
Isiah Haynes	Ryan Kelleher
Catherine M. Larkin	Maureen Martin
Rodney Moody	Susan Pasternack
Elli Stern	Cedric White
Karen White	Kyle White

Tom Brownscombe of the U.S. Chess Federation

A very special thanks to Joan M. Schlich, who became my own personal chess coach, mentoring me through a world that I knew very little about until I wrote this book. I am extremely grateful for her time, knowledge, and passion for this most amazing game.

For The Students Who Read *Stand Tall, Harry*

As each of you reads this book, I hope that it will help you to think about your classmates and how you treat each one of them. In every classroom there is probably going to be a Harry, a Jack, and a Tommy, and then, a you. I hope that this book will teach you not only about the many wonderful qualities of others, but a little about your wonderful qualities as well. To do this, you will need to open your mind and your heart. Once you do so, leave them open and they will serve you well as you grow into adulthood. Always "stand tall" and be proud of who you are. You can be anything you want to be in this life, as long as you are willing to work at it. Trust me, the doors will open.

You may notice that the chapters of this book have no titles. Every reader will have an idea about what might be best. If you are reading it in class, perhaps each student can think of a title for each chapter and you can vote to see which one seems the most appropriate. I look forward to hearing from you. Until then, happy reading!

Mary Mahony

Praise For
Stand Tall, Harry

" **A**n extraordinary achievement by the author to illustrate the impact that we have as individuals in shaping the lives of others, in particular, our children."
>   – Karen White, Parent

"*Stand Tall, Harry* clearly depicts the special bond that exists with intergenerational relationships. As a grandfather of twin boys, I'm truly moved by this story."
>   – Edward "Poppy" Burns

"The United States Chess Federation is pleased to endorse *Stand Tall, Harry* by Mary Mahony. Even though the author is not a chess player, she has done her homework. You'll have to wait until Ms. Mahony's next book to see whether Harry wins the tournament. But regardless of the result of the final game, Harry and all the other players in the King's K–12 Tournament are winners. Everyone who makes the effort to compete is a winner; the only losers are those who don't try."
>   – Tom Brownscombe
>   Director of Scholastic
>   Programs and Technical Affairs,
>   U. S. Chess Federation

Chapter One

The school I go to is way out in the country.

My school days are a lot different from those of the rest of the kids in my class. I get up at about six in the morning, do chores like making my bed and putting my lunch in my school bag, and then I sit down and look at a breakfast that I am too tired to eat. I sure would like to be in bed just a little bit longer. Even when my mom makes griddle cakes, I still would rather be in my bed. I walk to catch my school bus at the same time the joggers are coming home and old Mr. Peace is just back from walking his dog, Old Blue.

"Mornin', Mr. Peace."

"Mornin', Harry. Off to school are you now? Your mom and dad sure are giving you a good education. You're a lucky boy, that's for sure."

The school I go to is way out in the country, almost an hour from Boston on a good day, and usually over an hour and

fifteen minutes on a bad day. The bus ride is long and sometimes it seems as if we'll never get there. The bus goes along
the Charles River and then down some country roads. Some
mornings it looks like a big cloud is coming out of the river
and it's all kind of steamy. Over the river is the salt and pepper
bridge, my favorite. I call it that because it looks like salt and
pepper shakers from the table. And just when I think I'm
going to vomit because my stomach hates motion so much,
Mr. Barrett, our bus driver, says, "There's your future college,
kids. Harvard University is waiting for all of you!"

Harvard, schmarvard! Half the bus is just waking up. What
do I care about college? I'm only ten years old and I just want
to be like my friends in the city and go to a city school instead
of out in no-man's land. Even though I like hiking out where
my school is, I don't like it so much that I want to be there
every single day.

Our bus is almost always the last one to get to our school. I
hate walking into the cafeteria when all the other kids are
seated. My school is mostly White, only about fifteen of us are
Black. It's hard for the other kids to understand that it's weird
living in a neighborhood that is mostly Black and leaving it
each morning to go to a school that is mostly White. These are
the things you never talk about because you don't want to hurt
anyone's feelings, but it really is very weird. It's a lot easier
now than it was when I was in kindergarten. Back then I was
the only Black child in my grade. Now there are at least four
other Black students in fourth grade, so I'm a lot happier. Not
all of them live in Boston, but some of them do, and often they
ride my bus. My mom and dad know their parents so it's kind
of neat. Two of them go to my church and their moms sing in
the choir with my mom. But it's not cool to hang around with
your Boston friends if you want to make new ones.

I've been kind of waitin' for that one special school friend so
I can be part of the "in group." I often watch the other kids
and how they pal around with just one friend and I want to be
that way, too. Two of the other Black kids in my grade are
Leroy and David. They live in the same town that my school is
in so they do lots of stuff together. A few of the kids in my class
have been with me since kindergarten and I hang out with

them at recess, but I never see them after school. I've been over to their houses a few times, but they have never been to mine. I get tired of always going to where they live and doing what they want to do. One of them, Tommy, used to go to the reading teacher with me in first and second grade for extra help. He still has to go, but they told me that I am a great reader and that I just need to slow down. I used to skip words because I couldn't say them, but I pretended that I just didn't see them.

I kind of wish I still went to the reading teacher because then I could buddy-up with Tommy some more. I miss being his pal. Now he has a new one, Sam, who goes to the reading teacher with Tommy two days a week. Lately, Tommy kind of acts like he knows it all. That's silly because if Tommy knew it all, he wouldn't still need to see the reading teacher. But I guess the new kid likes that "know-it-all" stuff. I tried to help him a few times with his spelling, but Tommy just butted right in. He just has to know everything all the time! One day our teacher, Mrs. Lamont, even let the new boy choose his partner for spelling and, of course, he picked Tommy. I think she knew I was sad because she let me go to the office for her and I wasn't even the office messenger that week. When I got back I ended up being paired with a boy named Jack. He's never been in my class before which is really amazing since he's in the same grade. He's a pretty neat kid and I enjoyed doing spelling with him.

The person who I talk to the most is my big sister, Consuela. She's away at college now. My dad was married before, but his first wife died, and then he met my mom. Consuela was only two years old then, so my mom is now her mom, too. Consuela is a lot older than me, but it never seems like that. When she comes home from college, she takes me to special places like the Science Museum and we talk and talk and talk. She can look at something that seems boring and make it exciting. I love how she thinks. She's the one who really helped me with my math when it was getting hard. If I get a good report card, I'm going to be able to visit her at her college in Georgia. My Grampy says that it's a really "peachy" place and then laughs whenever he talks about Georgia, which is where peaches grow. It makes me think that Consuela is just sitting and eating peaches all day. I hope that's not true because I hate them. I don't like all that fuzz on the outside. It makes my throat itch. And how can you scratch your throat? Impossible! Ya know what I mean?

Each day when I get home from school, I see Mr. Peace giving Old Blue his afternoon walk. Sometimes it's beginning to get dark and I almost fall over them. There isn't anything blue about that dog, but I guess Mr. Peace thinks there is. My Grampy is always waiting on the top step of our house with a big smile on his face. I just love him so much. No matter how bad my day is, it never seems that bad once I see my Grampy. We always have all our big talks on the front step. He calls it his private office. I'm not sure what's so private about it since anyone walking by can see that we're out there, but maybe Grampy knows something about it that I don't. Grampy always looks me in the eye when our talks are done and says, "Stand tall, Harry. Be proud of who you are." Then he gives me a big hug and I feel so much better. I sure love him bigger than this whole world and I know he loves me the same.

Chapter Two

My neighborhood is very different from where I go to school. The houses are bigger and closer together. My Grampy and my parents all live in the same house and my Grampy has one house in that big house and we have the other. It's kind of like putting one flat house on top of another and making two, so it's really tall. People call them brownstones, meaning a special type of house. I wouldn't want you to think I live in a big brown rock!

Mr. Peace and his wife live next door, but they don't have family living in their other house because their son lives in Washington, D.C., and is a really famous person. My Grampy says he helps run our country. One of the families from our church lives in the other part of Mr. Peace's house now and they have kids my age. Well, almost! The only trouble is, they're both girls. Grampy says that I'll like them better later.

My friends live two streets over, and behind our houses is a big park that is next to a zoo. We always laugh at all the people who pay to get into the zoo because we just stand at the fence to see the animals. We used to go inside and have picnics when I was really little, but now you don't rock if you do that. My friends and I spend a lot of our time playing basketball at the park and going to Ken's Corner Store for our snacks. The park has lights now, but all our parents say that we have to be home before the lights go on. If you're still there when the lights appear, you're late for dinner, except in the summer. The park isn't the same at night and my parents tell me how dangerous it is to be there then. Even sometimes during the day, we leave if we see someone we don't know. The neighborhood rule is that you must always have a buddy in the park. My Grampy is really strict about that rule and he always asks me who I'm going to the park with. When I was little I used to play on the swings and jungle bars at the other end of the park. My mom told me that back then, as soon as someone got a new baby, they brought it to the park and all the other moms "oohed and aahed" about how cute the baby was. I guess you had to be there.

My mom used to play in the same park when she was little and Mr. Peace always tells me that my mom was one of the prettiest girls in the neighborhood. It's kind of weird thinking of your mom like that. Once, when someone got hurt at the park, they came looking for my mom because she's a nurse. She went right over and a few days later these people came to our house with a big basket of fruit and told my mom how great she was. I felt really proud and my Grampy was just beaming. He always says that my mom is just like her mom used to be. I never knew my Grammy because she died before I was born. I guess I'll just have to take my Grampy at his word.

My best friends are Hank and Herbie. My dad always calls us the three "H's." His favorite joke is, "Harry, which 'H' are you hanging out with today or are you hanging out with both 'H's'?" Then he just busts up laughing. I don't think it's that funny, but I guess my dad thinks it is. Parents can be very strange.

I don't get to see Hank and Herbie as much now. They both go to the school in our neighborhood and I have to go on that long bus ride out into the country. They have more friends here than I do now and we don't hang around as much as we used to. It's been kind of hard. We still play basketball together on Saturdays when I don't have hockey, and we still go to the same church, but it's different from what it used to be. I get home really late in the afternoon and they buddy-up to do school projects together after school. When I share things about my school, they always ask me when my school friends are coming to my house so they can meet them. I think they already know the answer. Sometimes I am mad that I can't go to the same school as they do.

My school friends don't seem to care very much about my friends at home. I want to know about *their* friends, but they never ask me about *mine*. Once I told them about how neat it was to live next to a zoo, and they just laughed and asked me if I feed the animals when I get home. My teacher heard them and was not happy. She had the whole class write out questions about the city and she asked me to write out questions about the country. I knew why she was doing it, but in a way I wished that she hadn't.

My mom explained to me that when you don't have to experience a change in your life, like leaving your city block and going to school in the country each day, it's hard to imagine what it is like. She's probably right, but that doesn't really help me a lot. Hank said that I should just tell my mom and dad that I don't want to go there. Herbie said I should act sick on the bus every day and say that I'm allergic to buses. Sometimes I think Herbie is allergic to thinking!

I started liking fourth grade a little more. The bus ride began getting easier because I had a few new bus friends. Some of them go to other schools in the same town that my school is in. One of them, Jeb, I really like a lot. He's a year older but we like a lot of the same stuff. In the beginning, we each complained about the bus ride, but then Jeb said, "One really neat thing, Harry, is that if we didn't ride this bus together, we might not be friends because I live in a different part of the city than you." Jeb was so right.

"Cool," I said. "Hey, this is a reason to like going to a different school."

Jeb and I ride to school together every day. If either of us gets sick, the other just sits alone holding the seat until the sick one comes back. Well, I don't mean "sick one" in a mean way. Oh, you know what I mean, don't you? The important thing is that thanks to Jeb, I began to have a whole new feeling about school. But I still didn't have a really special friend in my classroom. I gave up on the new boy because Tommy just hogged him all the time. He got right in his face.

I kind of liked Jack, you know, the kid I did my spelling with. We had a lot in common. Sometimes we played with our basketball cards at recess. He had a card for every single major NBA player, but I knew all their teams without even looking.

He'd never been to a pro game, so I told him that someday maybe he could go to one with my dad and me.

Since Tommy knew that Jack and I were starting to be friends, he started doing stuff that was kind of mean. One day he told Jack something that I didn't even say. Jack didn't believe him and that made me feel really good. Since then Jack and I became really special friends. In fact, we'd gotten so friendly that we made plans for me to go to Jack's house for an overnight and I hoped he'd visit mine in a few weeks. Jack said he really wanted to come to my house. If it's a nice weekend, we could get in some hoops over at the park or maybe at the Boys Club if it's not too crowded.

Today we had a half day and then there would be only one more day left until Friday, the day I would be off to Jack's house. I couldn't wait! I already had my bag packed, basketball cards and all.

Half days are crazy for me. Some of the kids from Boston stay home because they spend a good part of a half day on the bus going back and forth from the city. H. P. Junior and Celia, those are my parents, would never let me stay home on a half day. School, or that other long word they use that starts with the big "E" (education), is very important to them. You don't ever want to get my parents goin' on school. It's like church: a lot of sittin' and a *lot* of listenin'. Consuela told me that before she went off to college, and Consuela knows everything about our parents.

I was very excited about going to Jack's house and the chance to meet all his animals. Jack doesn't have any brothers or sisters but he has two rabbits, a dog, and goldfish. He writes about them in class all the time. His stories are very silly and they always make me laugh.

Sometimes I hear Mrs. Lamont say, "Jack, I need you to try to write about something that *really* happened."

When she says this, Jack just kind of shrugs his shoulders, smiles, and keeps writing his silly stories. He thinks of things that I would never think of and he makes them come alive, like walls and floors and stuff like that. In one of his stories a wall ate an NBA player while he was asleep in his bedroom and another player, who was not as good as the sleeping one, got to play in the next game. His last shot won the game and afterwards they found the really famous player behind his bedroom wall. Far-out stuff!

My dad went into work a little bit late today so he could see me off on the bus and make sure I had my gym bag packed with all the stuff I'd need for my overnight. Grampy offered to help, but Mom said she thought Dad should stick around to be sure Grampy didn't forget anything. Grampy gets confused sometimes and then he gets talkin' about Grammy and what a great "girl" she was and a few times I've missed my bus. The new thing is that Grampy only says good-bye to me from the steps, with no big morning talks. Then the only person who slows me down is Mr. Peace, although he knows I'm in a hurry, too. But Old Blue doesn't move out of the way for anybody. Not even for Mr. Peace!

Jeb was as excited as I was about my overnight and all the way to school we talked about what Jack and I would do. I showed Jeb some of my new basketball cards. He had some, too. I wish we went to the same school. I am always sad when we get off at different stops. His school isn't that far from mine but we don't do any stuff together. Jeb says that when I get to middle school we will get to see each other more.

I got to school late so I didn't get to talk to Jack. He had already gone down to our classroom with everybody else.

"Maybe we'll get to talk a little bit before Mrs. Lamont starts class," I thought to myself.

Tommy was out by the coat hooks, but everyone else was inside already.

"Hi, Harry! Why'd ya bring your gym bag to school?"

"Oh, hi, Tommy. I brought it because I'm going to Jack's house for an overnight and I am really excited! I'd like to talk more, Tommy, but I need to tell Jack something."

I rushed inside, but Tommy didn't follow me. I spotted Jack over in the library area of our classroom looking through some of the books. I raced over to him, but Mrs. Lamont announced that it was time to get back into our seats. I had just enough time to tell Jack that we'd talk at recess.

I thought I really aced my spelling test. The morning was just flying by and recess was in fifteen minutes. Jack kept looking over at me as if to say, "Is recess ever going to come?"

"Okay, children. Snack time," announced Mrs. Lamont. "Those of you who have forgotten to put your snacks in your desks may go out and get them now. I'm going to read another chapter to you from *Number the Stars* while you eat."

Then Susan came in and announced that her snack was missing from her backpack. Susan always brings in a special snack on Fridays and she always shows it to everyone and announces why she brought it. If Susan's snack was missing, Mrs. Lamont had a real problem on her hands.

A few minutes after Susan made her announcement I saw Tommy whisper something in Mrs. Lamont's ear. Then she came over to me and asked if she could look in my gym bag. Usually I didn't care who looked in my gym bag, but this time I got this creepy feeling in my stomach that maybe I *should* care.

The whole class watched when I went out of the room with Mrs. Lamont. Jack looked really sad for me. I took a quick look at my bag and I could see that it was half unzipped, and I knew that I had not left it like that, because of my basketball cards. When I began to unzip it the rest of the way, I was pretty sure that Susan's snack was sitting on top of my clothes. I could feel this big lump in my throat and I wanted to call my Grampy and tell him that I didn't do it. I knew my Grampy would believe me.

"Be proud of who you are, boy," I could hear him say these words over and over again.

As Mrs. Lamont took Susan's snack from my bag, I could feel her eyes looking for mine, but I didn't want her to see me.

"Harry, I don't think you did this and I think you know you didn't do this. Am I right, Harry?"

I couldn't talk. The words just wouldn't come out, so I just shrugged my shoulders. I went back into the room and Mrs. Lamont came in behind me and handed Susan her snack. I could see that everyone thought I had taken it. I wanted to run home I felt so bad. I couldn't even look at Jack. I felt as if every-one was staring at me. I only looked up once and I could see Tommy's eyes on me with this kind of grin on his face. I was so sad that I couldn't even be mad at him.

Mrs. Lamont started reading a chapter in *Number the Stars* to the class and most everyone began eating their snacks. Everyone but me. The lump in my throat was so big that I wondered if I would ever be able to eat again. I sure didn't want to go out to recess. Just when the lump in my throat became a knot in my stomach, the teacher from across the hall, Miss Hatzis, stuck her head in the door and asked Mrs. Lamont if she could see her right away.

Mrs. Lamont told us we could visit with each other while we finished our snacks and left the room to talk to Miss Hatzis. Usually the kids went crazy when she left the room, but today everyone was really quiet. I just kept my head down.

When Mrs. Lamont returned, she told us we were going to be late going out for recess because she wanted to talk to us about courage. Everyone looked very disappointed and most of the class turned to look at me. And then Mrs. Lamont said something that I will never, ever forget. Even when I am as old as my Grampy, I will remember this talk.

"Class, today Harry did something that took great courage and I want to share it with all of you," she began. "Someone put a snack in Harry's bag and blamed it on him. I know who that someone is because Miss Hatzis saw it all happen. It took great courage for Harry not to turn around and blame someone else. I hope that the person who made this mistake, and I'm sure it was a mistake, can also show courage and apologize to Harry for blaming him for something he did not do. And I also hope that this person has the courage to come to me in private. For now, I will apologize to Harry on behalf of that student. It takes a courageous student to do what Harry did, and again I want to tell Harry how sorry I am for all this. Recess will be a little shorter today. You can line up now to go out."

Chapter Three

*"I can't seem to fall asleep, which is really bothering
me 'cause I'm tired," I kept thinking to myself.*

Jack's house is not far from school. Usually his mom picks
him up at his babysitter's house at the end of the day, but
today his mom took the afternoon off from work. I could tell
that Jack was very excited. His mom would be taking us to
the ice cream store that is not far from our school and we
could order anything we wanted. I wanted a chocolate swirl
cone or a chocolate frappe, but I wasn't sure they'd have
them. I pretty much like any kind of ice cream, so if they
didn't, it was no big deal.

As I was racing out of school with Jack, something strange
happened. Tommy came running up to me and asked me if
he could talk to me alone for a minute. I really wanted to say
no, but he looked so sad that I said okay but that I only had a
minute because Jack's mom was waiting for us.

"Harry, I want you to know that I am very sorry for taking the snack and putting it in your bag. I am not sure why I did it. I guess sometimes I just do things like that."

I stood there for a minute and just looked at Tommy. I didn't know what to say and I was thinking of my Grampy. I wondered if anyone ever told Tommy to be proud of who he is, but I knew he would not have understood. I guess he was trying to stand tall by apologizing to me. I was also wondering why he did this in the first place. I couldn't understand because I have never taken anything from anybody.

"Hey, Harry. Over here. My mom is waiting for us."

I forgot that Jack was waiting for me. He was standing off by the wall while Tommy was talking to me. I was thinking about what Tommy had done and I forgot all about Jack.

"Coming," I called back. "Sorry, Tommy. Gotta go. Don't worry about the snack thing. I'm not mad at you but don't do it again. Okay?"

As I went racing over to Jack, I looked back and Tommy was standing all alone looking very sad. I was feeling bad for him; I'm not sure why. I knew Jack was waiting. I was really excited about going over to Jack's house and nothing was going to change that. I was also a tiny bit nervous.

"Hi, Harry. I'm Mrs. James, Jack's mom. We are very excited that you are spending the night with us."

"Me, too," I answered.

I was feeling a little weird. That whole snack thing was still kind of bothering me even though I tried not to think about it.

"Well, how about some homemade ice cream, guys?"

"Sounds good to me," Jack answered.

"Harry. C'mon. Let's have a race to the car. I see it over there."

While Jack and I raced to the car, his mom followed along behind us. I could hear her talking to the other moms and I had the feeling she knew a lot of the families at our school. It kind of reminded me of when we go to church and everyone talks to my mom or when my Grampy takes his afternoon walks around our neighborhood. We jumped in the car and took off. Before long I could see the ice cream store and Jack seemed as excited as I was.

"Can you tell just a little, Harry, that my Jack likes ice cream?" asked Mrs. James.

I liked her a lot already. She was kind of crazy and fun. She turned the music up in the car and started singing in this funny voice. The music was very strange. It kind of sounded like people were stretching their voices. Jack said it was something called "opera." I was a little confused because I thought she was the talk-show lady on TV who my Grampy watched and I didn't think that she was a singer, too. The *Oprah Winfrey Show* is one of my Grampy's favorites. Besides the news, it's the only show he sees during the day. I just kind of smiled and acted like I knew what they were talking about. I didn't feel nervous at all anymore.

The ice cream store was very neat. It was very different from my corner store, but not as nice as a Friendly's. There were only a few tables and most of them were full, so Jack grabbed two benches near the window and a chair for his mom. I ended up getting a banana smoothie, which was so good that I could have had two. Jack ordered a hot fudge sundae. His mom got frozen yogurt because Jack says ice cream makes her grow the wrong way.

We sat there for a long time just looking out the window, enjoying our ice cream and talking to Jack's mom. She wanted to know all about my family and if I had grown up and lived in Boston my whole life. I was so excited to talk to her about my family and where I lived and, of course, about my time with Grampy on the front step. It was the first time in a long while that I had a chance to really share what it was like where I lived. Best of all was that Jack's mom really listened to every word I said and even asked me more questions. I really liked her a lot.

After our ice cream, we went back to Jack's house. We were going to play outside in the fort he had made under his porch, but it started to rain really hard. His mom told us that it was not a "play outside" kind of day and so we went inside.

Jack's room looked so much like mine that for a minute I thought I was in my room and not his. Best of all, he had a chessboard and it was all set up on a Lego box waiting to be played. My dad, my Grampy, and I play chess all the time. My Grampy calls it a "thinker game." Each time he wins he puts a mark on the doorway into the kitchen. He's very proud of his tally marks. We leave the game up all the time and whoever wins gets to start off the next game. The loser has to wait one out since there are three of us and only two can play at a time.

Jack's board was all set up, too, and I could tell that he and someone else were in the middle of a game, because some of the chess pieces were in what my Grampy calls "strategic positions."

"Jack, who'd ya start this game with?" I asked.

"My dad, but he doesn't play as good as me, Harry, so he is always asking for a break so he can think about his next move. He just doesn't want me to beat him," Jack answered.

I laughed because it reminded me of my Grampy and my dad. I was kind of wishing that Jack and I could play, but I didn't say anything.

"Hey, Harry. Why don't you be my dad and finish his game with me. Want to?" Jack asked.

At first I felt a little bad taking over his dad's game, especially since I didn't even know his dad, but Jack seemed okay about it and I really wanted to play. It felt as if Jack and I sat at that chessboard for hours. Jack played a lot like me and was in no rush to finish 'cause he didn't want to lose. It gave us a chance to just rap about stuff. I really like having him as my friend. It's as if we've been friends for a long, long time.

All of a sudden I could feel someone standing over my shoulder. It was Jack's dad.

"Hi, Dad," said Jack. "This is Harry, the friend I was telling you about. Look, Dad, he's winning. He's a much better player than you, but that's okay, Dad. You're good at other games."

I felt kind of weird meeting his dad in his dad's chess seat. Mr. James just looked at us and laughed.

"Well, Harry, I guess it's a good thing you're a chess player because it's about time someone gave Jack some competition. He wins every single game, Harry."

Chapter Three

We all started laughing and in the background Jack's mom was calling us for dinner. On the way to school I had worried that I might not like the dinner, but I wasn't even thinking about it. I was having so much fun that a meal wasn't such a big deal.

Dinner was pretty wild at Jack's. His dog, Freeway, had this funny shade on his head because he had just had surgery. He had swallowed a piece to one of Jack's games and they had had to operate. I guess Freeway could have died. Jack's mom kept saying, "poor baby," and as soon as Freeway got near the table, Jack's dad ordered him back to his dog bed. Then Jack's mom would start again, "poor baby," and the whole scene would happen all over.

"Harry, this goes on at every meal. Pretty crazy stuff, huh?" Jack laughed.

I couldn't help but laugh with him. Especially when Freeway started howling in the corner. It was like something out of a sitcom on TV. It was one of the funniest dinners I ever had. More laughing than eating.

After dinner Jack and I played with Sigmund, the bigger of his two rabbits. Sigmund had been at our feet through much of dinner. I could not believe that Freeway didn't bother Sigmund, but he didn't. Jack explained that Sigmund had the run of the house because he was trained to use the litter box in the back hall. The other rabbit, Snickers, had to stay in the cage. Snickers wasn't litter box–trained.

Finally, it was time to go to bed. I was pretty tired. Besides, I had never slept in bunk beds before and Jack said I could sleep on the top if I wanted. I sure did want! I couldn't wait to get up there. Jack and I talked for a while and then all of a sudden there were no more words coming from the bottom bunk. Just a lot of snoring. Jack reminded me of my dad even though Jack is a lot younger.

"I can't seem to fall asleep, which is really bothering me 'cause I'm tired," I kept thinking to myself. I began worrying about Tommy and what happened in school. I kind of wished that I had ridden the bus home so I could have talked to Jeb about it. I knew he would understand, because sometimes on the bus we talk about getting blamed for things we don't do. It happens to all kids I guess, but being a Black kid in an all-White school sometimes makes it even harder.

I was still feeling really sad for Tommy. He looked so alone when I left with Jack. Kids can be really tough. I wasn't sure why he did it and I guess he didn't know either. I just hoped nothing like that *ever* happened to me again.

Not being able to fall asleep was making me homesick.

"I sure do miss my own bed," I thought to myself. I had never had an overnight before except with my friends in Boston. I just really, really wanted to fall asleep.

"Hey, Harry, knock yourself out. You've been sleepin' all morning and I want to do some stuff. We're gonna miss the whole day, Harry."

I opened one eye and there was Jack with his dog, Freeway, waiting for me to wake up. I looked at my watch and I couldn't believe my eyes. It was ten o'clock. I got out of bed so fast that I missed the ladder and almost landed on Freeway. The dog went yelping into the kitchen and Jack and I got into such a laugh that I thought I would never be able to stand up.

I quickly got dressed and did all my bathroom stuff. Jack's mom was in the kitchen making me griddle cakes. Jack and his parents called them pancakes. They smelled s-o-o-o good. Grampy is the pancake maker in our house and we call them "Grampy's griddle cakes, the best in Boston."

After breakfast we walked down to the five-and-ten-cent store to get some more basketball cards. We met Tommy on the way. He was coming back all by himself and he looked so lonely. I asked Jack if we could talk to him for a few minutes. Tommy said he couldn't play with anyone because of what he had done at school. It made me really sad for him.

I loved the old five-and-ten-cent store. It was a real country store. The floors were very uneven and it had stuff in it that looked like things they used in the olden days. I could have wandered around there all day long. The candy section was far-out. We each got a pack of basketball cards and some Dots and gum. We took our time going back to Jack's because we knew my mom and dad would be picking me up and we wanted more time to play. I had a hockey practice in the afternoon that I couldn't miss. Well, I suppose I could, but my coach would be smokin' he'd be so fired up about me not thinking of the team. He says that when you're on a team, you each depend on one another. He calls it "teamwork."

"Harry, looks like you might want to just move in and live at Jack's house."

My mom was sitting at Jack's kitchen table having a cup of tea with his mom when we came in. My dad was out in Jack's garage helping Mr. James move a grill. It was as if Jack and I had known each other our whole lives.

"Jack, we'd like you to come to Boston for an overnight some weekend soon so we can show you our town," said my mom. "It's a little bigger than this, but our neighborhood has the same feeling minus all the woods and big yards. You and Harry can figure out a good time to do it."

"Oh, thanks, Mrs. Jones. I'd love to come," Jack answered. "My mom grew up in New York City and we go to Boston a lot."

"I think Jack is ready to come with us now, Harry. Unfortunately, it won't work out today. Jack has plans and so do we," said my mom.

I was kind of disappointed, but my mom was right. I wanted Jack to meet Herbie and Hank and go over to the zoo with us. I couldn't wait. He would be the first school friend to come to my house for a sleepover.

Chapter Four

The ride home from Jack's was kind of, well, very quiet. I had the feeling that my mom and dad wanted to talk to me about something. When I got home my Grampy was sitting on the front step with the same kind of look on his face. As my mom passed by my Grampy, I heard her say, "Don't mention a thing."

After I gave my Grampy the bear shake that he always waits for, I rushed into my bedroom to unpack and get ready for hockey. My dad followed me in.

"You okay, son? Mrs. Lamont called yesterday and told us about the snack incident and Tommy. She felt really bad about it, Harry. She told us you had courage and never accused anybody. But how come you never told her that you didn't do it, son?"

"I don't know, dad. I was so upset that I couldn't even think. But the upset part was all inside me. Everybody just kept staring. I kept thinking about what Grampy always says, 'Stand tall, Harry. Be proud of who you are.' Once I thought I might cry, but just when I thought I would, Mrs. Lamont talked to the class and I felt better. But I didn't like everyone looking my way and I still didn't know why it all happened, anyhow."

"You know, son, we live in a world where there are a lot of unhappy people, children and adults. I don't think Tommy meant to do this, but I think that maybe he was having a hard time and it just happened."

"I know, Dad. That's what he told me when he said he was sorry. I felt really sad for him because I don't think he has many friends. When I used to go to reading with him, I really liked Tommy, Dad, but this year he didn't seem to want to be my friend anymore. He's friends with the new boy in class."

"Harry, I think that perhaps he does want to be your friend. Maybe it's hard for him to see you finding a new friend in

Jack. Or maybe, Harry, it was for a reason that is inside Tommy that has nothing to do with you. The important thing, son, is that you made us proud. Always be proud of who you are."

I was eating my dinner when the doorbell rang and I could hear Hank and Herbie in the back hall talking to Grampy, who was raving about my mom's collard greens and offering Herbie and Hank some. Herbie calls collard greens "wilted grass," so I knew he wasn't too happy about Grampy's offer. The barbecued chicken would be a lot more appealing to him.

"Hey, Harry, how was the overnight?" they both asked me at almost the same time.

"Awesome, guys. So cool. Jack might be coming down here next weekend to hang out with us."

"Neat. You know they are having a big sports day at the Boys Club so maybe he can come along," said Hank.

"I know Jack likes basketball so maybe we can get a game going," I replied.

"We can always just go to your hockey game, Harry, and hang out and eat," added Herbie.

"Sounds good to me," I replied. "Listen, guys. I have a hockey practice so I can't go out with you to rent the movie like we had planned. They changed our practice time because they can't get the ice tomorrow afternoon. I can't do the Wednesday practice because of school. My dad says I get too tired and he can't pry me out of bed the next morning."

"That's what happens, Harry, when you leave your buddies and go to a country school," ragged Hank.

"That's what you guys always say. Well, that's where my school is and I'd be tired no matter because hockey is such a workout. Besides, I get two sets of friends and I am really starting to like my school more and more."

"Time to go, Herbie. Joe Cool is getting into himself. See you later, Harry."

"Yo! Listen, guys. Stop giving me a hard time and thanks for coming over. Maybe I'll see you tomorrow."

I raced through the rest of my dinner and quickly got into my hockey uniform, grabbing my gear on the way out the door. My Grampy and my dad were waiting in the car.

Chapter Four

"Those boys sure do give you a hard time, Harry. You handle yourself pretty well."

My Grampy always had something good to say about everything. I knew what was coming next.

"Stand tall, Harry. Be proud of who you are." My Grampy has said those words to me ever since I can remember. Even if he's watching the news on the TV and he sees someone being mistreated, he says, "People have to stand tall and be proud of who they are." These are the words that my Grampy lives by. He grew up when people were not nice to Blacks. He once told me that he wasn't allowed to go into the corner store and buy his own ice cream because he was Black and no Blacks were allowed in the store. He used to ask a White friend of his to do it for him. Once, the White friend brought Grampy into the store and the owner kicked both of them out. It's hard for me to know what it was like to live like my Grampy did. I am so proud to have him as my Grampy and I can't understand how anyone could have treated him like that. As my teacher would say, he is a good citizen and he has a lot of courage. He's the best. To me he stands as tall as the Prudential Tower in Boston. He is my giant of a Grampy.

As we pulled into the rink parking lot, my dad did his usual groaning about how hard it was going to be to park. It wouldn't be a night at the rink without a groaning dad. He's much happier when my mother stays home because as soon as he starts the parking-lot groan, she says, " H. P. Junior, that's not a parking-lot groan I hear, is it? If you saw some of my patients you would see that being challenged about finding a parking space is no reason to groan. Now if you are sick, you just might have a reason to groan."

My dad always responds by saying, "Thank you, Nurse Jones."

I think it's pretty funny. Most of the time my parents remind me of newlyweds. My dad is always telling my Grampy that my mother is his most beautiful daughter. The fact of the matter is, she is my Grampy's *only* daughter!

As I walked into the rink, I was still smiling about my dad. The icy chill of the rink certainly got me into the hockey mode. I quickly put my skates on and got out on the ice. I play defense, not the easiest position, but it is so "hot" to be the first one on the ice. You feel like you're standing on a giant mirror that is watching every move you make. Hockey is a game I love more than anything I do, except maybe math and chess, and then basketball. Sometimes, when I lose a hockey game, I dream of being a famous chess king and then the losing doesn't seem to be such a bad thing. My dad always says, "Make sure you have lots of choices in life, Harry."

Chapter Five

The bus ride home was quiet
and I dozed for most of it.

"**H**arry Jones. Where are you, boy? It's almost time for the bus."

"Okay, okay. I'm coming. I was just getting something in the kitchen. I'll be right out," I called to my mom.

She had worked the night shift at the hospital and was ready for her sleep but wanted to get me out first. I almost liked it better when Grampy was in charge. He was more laid-back about getting out on time. A few times he was so laid-back that I missed the bus!

I raced down the steps and almost landed on Mr. Peace's dog. Old Blue was not happy and I'm pretty sure I heard a growl.

"Sorry, Old Blue. I'm late today."

Do you know how many times I have landed on that dog? Plenty.

"Never mind, son, just make that bus," said my dad. "Your mom needs to get her sleep."

Just as I came around the corner the bus was pulling away. All of a sudden it stopped short and the door opened. Boy, was I relieved. I could see Jeb in the back laughing. I knew he had yelled for Mr. Barrett to stop.

"You owe me one, Harry. That was pretty close," laughed Jeb.

"Thanks, Jeb. My mom would sure let me know what she thinks about me being late today. The whole block would know about it. She had a busy night at the hospital and was pretty grumpy this morning."

I spent almost the whole ride telling Jeb about my sleepover at Jack's. He was very excited for me. He has a friend from his school that he's known since kindergarten. He met him when the boy's family became Jeb's host family. They do everything together, including going to the same soccer camp during the summer. Each Halloween they take turns going to each other's neighborhood: One year they go to the country and the next year they go to the city.

As I was getting off the bus at school, I remembered that I hadn't told Jeb about what had happened in class on Friday with Susan's snack. Somehow it didn't seem that important anymore. I hoped it would never happen again. Besides, my dad always says we need to move on and so I decided it really was old news.

Jack was waiting for me in the cafeteria when our bus got in. Most of the classes had already left, but somehow Jack got to hang around for me. I told him about my hockey game and about how excited I was about him coming to my house. I was hoping that it might work out for the next weekend.

My school day seemed so long. Mondays are always like this, but this one seemed really, really long. I was kind of sleepy, maybe because I was so excited about Jack that I wasn't able to unwind. It was raining outside and the clouds were making my eyes droopy. It seemed like snack time was never going to come. I had a few Starbursts in my pocket from Grampy. I wondered if I could sneak one in my mouth to recharge my battery. Grampy always says sugar recharges your battery, so that's why he needs extra dessert. My mom always adds, "And more cavities, too!" I guessed I could just pass on the candy and wait.

When it was time for snack, I looked over and Tommy was just sitting there without anything to eat. Mrs. Lamont always has crackers to share, but today Tommy just sat there and didn't even ask for some. I think he was afraid to draw attention to himself because of what he had done to me on Friday. After a few minutes, I reached in my desk and got out the second snack that I had grabbed from my kitchen at the last minute. I almost missed the bus because of it. I walked over to Tommy's desk and gave it to him. I could feel everyone watching me.

Tommy began to push it away and I whispered, "Please take it 'cause I brought it just for you."

He raised his head up just a little and I could see a smile deep in his eyes.

"Thank you, Harry," he whispered.

As I started back to my seat, Mrs. Lamont looked up from the book she was reading and gave me a big, warm smile.

After snack my day really picked up. Since I already knew most of my times tables, I was doing some "think math" problem cards. Some of them are really hard and sometimes I spend my whole math time just trying to find the answer to one problem. Some of the problems have more than one step. Those are the really tricky ones and I know when I get one of those answers right, I might really become a math whiz some day. I think it would be neat to be a math whiz. I think about that a lot.

We had indoor recess because it rained the rest of the morning. Jack and I played a game that we found on the game shelf, but mostly we just talked about how much fun we had at the sleepover. Jenny kept coming over so she could hear what we were saying, but we stopped talking each time we saw her approaching us. Finally, she told me that she thought it was nice of me to give Tommy some snack. Jack thanked her for me and finally she left us alone. Girls!

The bus ride home was quiet and I dozed for most of it. Jeb had after-school sports and anyway, I was very tired. Mr. Barrett kept asking me questions since the bus was pretty empty, but I didn't remember answering him because I fell asleep as we were getting on the highway heading home.

"Wake up, son. Wake up! Time to get off," said Mr. Barrett.

"What's he gonna do?" I mumbled.

"What are you talking about, son? The only thing he's gonna do is get you off his bus so he can get on home to his wife and his slippers! Now, come on, Harry. Wake up son!"

The next thing I knew I was running off the bus so fast that my feet never touched the steps. Mr. Barrett was laughing so hard that if I had turned around I might have seen the bus shaking. It sure was a long ride going from my school all the way home to Boston.

At dinner, we all talked about Jack coming for the weekend. We decided to invite him to my hockey game on Saturday and then he could stay over after that. My mom leaves for work on Fridays just about when school gets out and Grampy watches me until my dad gets home. Grampy doesn't drive. He always says that's what feet are for. I would have no way of getting Jack to Boston because we are not allowed to have friends ride the bus with us and both of Jack's parents work. My dad said that my mom would call Jack's mom in the morning. I was so excited I could hardly do my homework.

About eight o'clock there was a knock at the door. It was Herbie. At first my dad told him it was too late for one "H" to see another "H," but finally he let Herbie in. As soon as I saw Herbie's face, I knew something was up.

"Herbie, what are you doin' out so late? I didn't think my dad was goin' to let you in!"

"Harry, I hate my new class. There's no Hank in it. I miss Hank. I know lots of the kids, but it's not like it used to be and I'm gettin' down about it. I was sure Hank would be in my class and now he's gone just like you're gone. He's way down the hall and I almost never see him. He even went and found a new "H," Henry, after we all promised there would only be three

Chapter Five

"H's." I don't want to meet some new dude named Henry. What's the matter with him, Harry?"

I always thought I would be the one having these problems, not Herbie. I was the one who had gone way out of Boston to school. Herbie was always giving me a hard time about going out of my own "backyard" and leaving everything that was "hip hop," as Herbie would say.

Herbie and I ended up sitting on my front step and rapping about just about everything in Herbie's school day. I told him that when I first went out to the burbs to school, I missed the three "H's" so much that my stomach hurt. It was so easy in Boston and so hard out there. Each year I tried to find someone new and finally I found Jack who, even though he's a "J" and not an "H," is pretty cool.

"So, Herbie, dude, it's okay to add another 'H' because I'm adding a 'J.' Ya know, Herbie, my dad says that there are two sides to everything and you have to work a little harder at making some new friends. Kids are not just gonna jump out of some locker and say, 'Whoa, Herbie. Whassssssup man! Wanna be my friend?'"

Herbie and I started to laugh so hard that my dad heard us.

"Harry, Herbie. Do you know what time it is? Now, Herbie, you need to go on home, boy, before your mama calls me looking for you. This is a school night, son."

Herbie quickly left while I got ready for bed in record time.

"Dad, Dad, it's okay. I was just helping Herbie out with some school stuff. He was really missing me in school so I was making him feel better."

"Okay, son, just don't tell your mama I let you stay up so late. Have a good sleep, son. Maybe Herbie needs to hang out with you and your friend Jack this weekend."

"Thanks, Dad. Love you. See you in the morning."

"Not if I see you first, son!"

My dad, the comic. He always has a comeback and you can always hear my Grampy say in the background, "That used to be my material!"

Chapter Six

I began getting ready for school earlier and earlier and at night I packed an extra snack for Tommy so I wouldn't be late getting it in the morning. I didn't do it every night, because I knew my mom would see that snacks were leavin' her kitchen much too fast. Being a nurse, my mom is really into eating good stuff and not too much of the other kind.

When I got on the bus, Jeb was waiting for me holding a seat in our favorite spot, the back of the bus. I couldn't wait to tell him about Jack coming down for the weekend and I wanted to rap with him about Herbie, too.

"Hey, man, whasssup Harry?"

Jeb was so cool and sometimes he really could make a whole bus laugh. In the background I could hear everyone echoing Jeb with one big, long "whasssup." Even though we are all different ages, our bus is like a family, one of those extended ones that goes from Boston to the burbs. Really, it is more like going into the woods for school. Our school is way, way out. There are kids on my bus that I would never have met in Boston. We are all trying to do good stuff in a town that we are trying to connect to, at least from Monday to Friday. On the weekends, it's tough because it is so far out of Boston and getting to the activities is not very easy. What a lot of people in the burbs do not understand is that when you live in Boston, you don't always need to own a car. Parking is not so easy and you can get a bus to almost anywhere in town. Most families are starting to own at least one car, but you really don't have to. I already told you what my Grampy does. He still points to his feet and says, "These are still the only free fare around."

I quickly slid into the seat next to Jeb just as Mr. Barrett was pulling away.

"Jeb, guess what? I think Jack is coming to my house on Saturday for an overnight. Mom is going to call and ask his mom today. I'm pretty excited. He can come to my hockey game and hang out with Hank and Herbie and probably this Henry dude, too. Jeb, if you want to meet him, you could even come."

"Whoa, whoa. Play it back a little. Since when did you add another 'H'?"

"Well, I'm not sure because I haven't talked to Hank yet, but Herbie seems to think we have a new 'H.' There's this new kid, Henry, who is in Hank's class, and Herbie thinks that Henry is getting to be pretty tight with Hank. Herbie's feeling pretty bad about this kid. Herbie really unloaded with me about it last night. He didn't want anyone new messin' with the three 'H's.' I told him that I had added a 'J' for Jack and so another 'H' wasn't the end," I began.

"Herbie's feeling kind of left out. He's got all these kids in his class that he doesn't hang out with and his class is way down the hall from Hank's. This is the first year they have been separated, so it's bad news for Herbie. He doesn't like his teacher, either, but I think that maybe he does but he's on one of his I-don't-like-anything-anyone trips. Herbie can get like that when things aren't going his way. Hank and I keep him upbeat, but if we aren't around, oh boy, you just better watch out! He's the youngest of four boys and they are always diggin' at him. I like them okay but I wouldn't want all those brothers, that's for sure."

"Well, listen, Harry," said Jeb. "Maybe you ought to get Herbie and Hank together and talk about this. Sounds like they aren't gonna be friends if you don't get in there."

"You're probably right, Jeb. I guess I was hoping that Herbie would come around and that maybe Hank, Herbie, Henry, Jack, and I could all be friends. Ya know what I mean?"

"Oh, sure, I know what you mean, but I think you're a dreamer, Harry. Herbie is asking for some help and Hank is probably mad that he's acting kind of strange about this new dude, Henry. And Henry probably needs Hank the way Herbie needs Hank so it sounds like some pretty complicated stuff is goin' on."

"Well, maybe. I'm just so excited about Jack that I'm not thinking about the 'H's' right now. I guess I'd better, or else adding a 'J' is also gonna mean really big trouble. I want to make sure everyone is nice to Jack and makes him feel good about being with us."

Just as I finished my sentence, the bus was pulling up to the back door of my school. Students are like trained seals when it comes to getting on and off a bus. The person who counts how many times they do this in a lifetime could probably get some prize for keepin' count. Mr. Barrett takes his schedule very seriously and he always makes sure when the bus stops that you go out of there with whatever you got on with. He knows everything about you and your family going way back. I think he's the king of Boston 'cause he sure knows a lot.

"Boys, boys. I need you to do the other kind of rapping. You just wrap yourself around the seat and move on out of this bus," said Mr. Barrett. "I got people waitin' on me."

"See you later, Jeb," I called. "Thanks for helping me out with this stuff."

I was so excited to find Jack and tell him about the overnight that I missed the last two steps out of the bus and hit the ground with a thud. I felt kind of silly but just got up, grabbed my backpack, and ran into school. Sure enough, we were the last bus in. Boy, that really bugged me. As I came around the corner and entered the main hallway, I spotted Jack on his way to the office.

"Jack, Jack. My mom is calling yours today to see if this weekend will be okay."

"Harry, I thought maybe you were sick or something. You're bus is really late today."

"I know we're really late. There was an accident in Boston and the traffic was backed up," I explained to Jack. "I was so busy talking to my friend Jeb that I didn't pay much attention to it. Jeb's a fifth grader and goes to the middle school. We sit together every day. It's kind of like sitting with a buddy on a field trip. The only trouble is, we do the same field trip every day!"

"Boys, I need you in your seats," came the voice of Mrs. Lamont. "We are about to start our morning exercises."

Mrs. Lamont says the same thing at almost the same time every morning. She has a funny accent and often talks about her school days in Tennessee where she grew up. She has made sure that we all know where Tennessee is on the map. Some of the kids still can't find Massachusetts, but they know right where Tennessee is.

Just as we were about to begin the Pledge of Allegiance to the flag, Tommy came racing into the room. He looked like he had just gotten out of bed. Mrs. Lamont put the rest of us on hold and quickly got him in his seat and ready to begin his day. I looked over at him and smiled. I really wanted to be friends. The snack thing was long gone and my Grampy was right about not gettin' stuck on stuff. Grampy always says, "If you give a little, you'll get a little back, and then a little more and a little more."

Before we knew it, it was time for recess, and Jack and I were almost the first in line. I couldn't wait to plan our weekend and I was hoping Jack could come. By the time we got to the double doors leading out to the playground, we had it all planned. Jack would watch my hockey game and hang out with Herbie so Herbie wouldn't feel left out if Hank hung out with Henry. Got that? After the game, we'd stay at the rink for a while and see what game was after ours. Then, maybe my mom and dad would let us watch a movie over at Hank's. One of his brothers works at a video store and he can bring home any movie for free because the owner likes him. He is only allowed to borrow them for two days. Of course, they are always PG. That is absolutely all we are allowed to see and our parents are really strict about that. Hank says that if his brother ever brought home an R movie, he'd have to go RRRRRight out the door with it!

Just as we were lining up to go back in from recess, we both noticed Tommy standing all alone over by a tree.

"Hey, Jack, how about we go tell Tommy it's time to line up," I said.

Jack knew what I was thinking right away.

"Okay, sure. But do you think he'll get mad that we're telling him what to do?"

"I don't think so. Especially if it's me because of the snack stuff."

"Hey, Tommy," I called out. "Want to walk in with us?"

"No, you guys want to be alone so it's okay," he weakly called back.

"Hey, Tommy. If we wanted to walk in alone, I wouldn't have called out to you. Come on in with us. Jack is tired of talking to me and wants to talk to someone else."

Slowly Tommy came over to us. Jack was great and just kind of kidded Tommy into joining us by asking him for some chess help. It was pretty funny since Tommy doesn't play chess. Jack loves chess so much that he doesn't even care if someone understands the game. He'll just barrel on into his chess-talk mode, sometimes on fast-forward, which really loses kids. When he's all done, the kid will say, "Is chess a game or something?"

Then Jack gets this really mixed-up look and says, "Oh, sorry! Yeah, it is. It's a game."

"Jack, I think my brain is on stop when it comes to games like chess," Tommy answered.

Jack was just starting his anyone-can-play speech when Mrs. Lamont said that recess was over. Jack just sort of left Tommy off in the middle of his sentence, kind of like, "You keep talking but I have to hang up." Tommy gave me this confused look and we both laughed.

"Tommy, Jack raps about chess so much that sometimes he forgets who he's talking with 'cause he's so into the move. I think it's kind of funny, but maybe that's because I play, too. You probably think we're chess nerds. Maybe I can show you how to play sometime and then we won't look so 'nerdy' to you!"

"Boys, please. Get into your seats," Mrs. Lamont called out. "It's time for *Scholastic News.*"

It was Tommy's job to be the "paper passer," and when Mrs. Lamont handed him the Scholastic newspapers, he cracked up laughin'.

"Tommy, Tommy. If you can't control yourself, I'll get someone else to pass them out. Recess is over."

Jack got his paper next and I could see him giggling. When I got mine, I just let go with a belly laugh. The title of the front-page article was "Chess Nerds Go International."

"Tommy, Jack, Harry," said Mrs. Lamont. "Do you mind telling me what is so funny about this article? I am surprised at you, Jack and Harry, because both of you love chess."

"That's just it," Tommy yelled out. "They're chess nerds!"

"Tommy, that'll be enough," Mrs. Lamont scolded.

"No, wait, Mrs. Lamont," I spoke up. "Tommy is right. I told him that Jack and I are chess nerds on the way in from recess, so when we all saw the article it was a crack-up."

"Well, to me a crack-up is a car accident, so why don't we all settle down and Harry, why don't you start the reading."

I had a hard time switching gears and getting serious, but finally I did and the article was pretty neat. All these chess nerds were going to an international chess tournament in a big plane to some place in Europe. Definitely something I could see myself doing. The amazing thing was that some of them were fourth and fifth graders. I was really getting into this and I knew Jack was, too, because even when the class moved to the article on the next page, we both kept reading the chess story. I couldn't wait to bring the story home and show my dad.

When it was time for lunch, Jack and I got in the front of the line since it was pizza day. Tommy snuck in right behind us, which didn't make the girl that he cut off happy. Finally she let him in and didn't tell Mrs. Lamont. When Jack and I got our pizza, we sat at the first table so we could eat while the pizza was hot. Pizza is like flat rubber when it cools and the cheese peels off, almost like you have two layers, one cheese and the other damp bread. Tommy came out just as we were sitting down. He kept looking around holding his tray and I could tell he had no one to sit with. He sits alone a lot. Just as the lunch-room aide was going over to tell him to hurry up and sit, I waved to him to come to our table. I knew we wouldn't be able to talk much about the weekend, but I felt kind of bad for him having to eat alone. I had done it many times, myself, and it didn't feel good at all. Some things you never forget. Jack looked surprised when my arm went up, but then he saw Tommy coming and he knew what I had done.

"Thanks, guys. You can keep on talking about your chess stuff; I'll just eat my pizza."

"Tommy, wasn't that funny about the chess nerds this morning?" I said.

"It was so funny, Harry. I was really busting up inside and Mrs. Lamont just didn't get it, did she?"

"Oh, I think she got it but she was trying to keep us . . ." And before I could finish Jack yelled out "on task" and we all started laughing.

We spent our whole lunch talking about chess and when it was time to go out on the playground, another fourth-grade teacher was blowing the whistle to go in. I didn't even care because we had so much fun at lunch. I really liked having Tommy eat with us and I think Jack did, too. Tommy is really an okay kid.

My school week was finally ending and the next day Jack would be coming to Boston. He was out sick Wednesday, but he came back Thursday with just a little cough. I really couldn't wait for him to see where I live and especially for him to meet my Grampy. Hank and Herbie promised to hang out with Jack while he watched my hockey game. The rink where the game would take place is part of a big university in Boston, and when I go there, I get to see the college kids play. They are always high-fiving us. It's kind of a cool rink and the ice is really fantastic. They have a big refreshment area, too. It would be pretty sweet, having all my friends there watching me play. The team we'd be playing is pretty tough to beat so I hoped our team was up for them. I really wanted to play my best and let Jack see what hockey is all about. Basketball is kind of his thing so he doesn't know a lot about hockey. If Herbie decided to be the hockey expert, which he sometimes does, I'd be in real trouble. One of Herbie's brothers plays college hockey and Herbie doesn't like hockey very much because this brother used to pick on him a lot. If Herbie got on one of his I-hate-hockey trips, he'd probably give Jack his 101 reasons why he doesn't play, instead of helping Jack figure out what I was doin' out there.

Stand Tall, Harry

I was having a lot of trouble keeping my mind on school and Jack kept looking over at me, smiling, with this big grin on his face. I could tell he was really excited about coming over, which made me feel good. I love where I live and I haven't been able to share it with too many kids in my school. A few times when I invited kids over, the day before they were supposed to come they canceled and said it was too far for their parents to drive. I wanted to say, "But I come to your place every day for school, so what's the problem?" I never said anything. Instead, I just felt bad.

"Harry. Harry Jones. Have you started your weekend already? It's your turn to read, Harry. First paragraph, top of page 22. Do you remember? We're reading about the Resistance and Denmark."

I could feel my face turning color, which may have been hard for others to see, but I sure knew it. I could feel myself stumbling over the words because my mind was not quite there yet. I was still on overnights.

Finally, Mrs. Lamont called on someone else for the next paragraph. I was glad because today I just wanted the bell to ring. And at long last, it did!

Chapter Seven

"This boy may need to be admitted."

I think my whole house got up when it was still dark out this morning. Everyone was so excited about Jack coming. I could hear Grampy outside sweeping the steps which was pretty funny since it rained last night. All my favorite smells were coming from the kitchen, which told me that my mom was cooking up a storm. The vacuum was going and my mom was telling my dad in a loud voice, so he could hear her over the vacuum-cleaner sound, to do a good job. Then the phone rang and I was sure it was my sister, Consuela, since she always calls on Saturday mornings. I could hear my mom telling her that I wanted to talk to her, because my mom didn't want to tell her what was really happenin' here. It was all very funny.

We have people here all the time so what's the big deal? It's the "first-time visit" scene. My mom has this thing about first-time visitors. I remember when the pastor of our church came. My dad said he should have been a pastor, because my mom made such a big deal of the visit. Grampy said it was a mom thing, but he also said, "Better not share this with your mom!"

I think it's really a mom and dad thing because my dad helps get ready for the visits, too. If the President of the United States ever came, I bet my parents would spend a year getting ready!

Even though it was kind of damp outside, I sat on the front step waiting for Jack so his parents would know they had the right house. The numbers in the front are pretty big and they could probably find it easily enough, but I wanted to be the first to greet Jack.

I was hoping Hank and Herbie didn't stop by until after lunch. I wanted to show Jack around the neighborhood on my own first.

Jack's dad has an old maroon Volvo that has stickers from, as Mrs. James says, "Places he dreams of going but hasn't been yet!" Each time Jack's dad hears about someone going on vacation to one of these places, he asks for a window sticker. After he puts it on the window, his dad makes a big deal of it, as if they actually went there. The fact of the matter is, they didn't! Sounds like something *my* dad would do.

"Jack, Jack!" I shouted. "Over here. Just have your dad park in our driveway."

"Mom, Dad. Jack and his parents are here. Grampy, Jack's here!"

"Calm down, Harry. Calm down, boy, or the whole neighborhood will be at our doorstep," yelled my mom as she came racing out the door, with her apron still on.

As I raced down the steps to meet them, I almost knocked over old Mr. Peace, who was taking Old Blue for his late-morning walk. Old Blue started hollering up a storm and everyone began laughing. It was a pretty silly sight but one thing was for sure: Old Mr. Peace was more confused than ever. Finally, Grampy explained why I was so excited and he even asked Mr. Peace to join us for lunch. I didn't think my mom was too thrilled about that, but, luckily, Mr. Peace decided Old Blue would be better off outside finishing his walk.

Finally we went inside and Mom and Dad showed Jack's parents up to our apartment, but not without Grampy showing off his apartment first and making his usual jokes about being an old bachelor now since my Grammy had died.

Lunch went on forever and by the time dessert came, everyone looked like they were in pain from eating so much. As we were finishing up, Jack's dad asked if he and Jack's mom could get a tour of the neighborhood and maybe take a walk. Within five minutes we had left the dishes on the table and were all outside walking around the zoo and then over to the park. Grampy was so proud and shared things about the history of where we lived that I had never heard before. We learned that Jack's dad had driven a truck during summers when he was in college and knew quite a bit about the streets. He told us that at that time he was one of the only White people delivering 'cause it was when Whites and Blacks didn't mix much, which is a pretty silly thing, not to mix just because of your color. Whoever thought of that rule? Couldn't have been a very smart person.

When the walk was over, it was time for me to get ready to head over to the rink for my hockey game. Herbie had already called twice and Hank was due to call any minute. While my mom cleaned up the kitchen with Grampy sort of helping (I knew he wanted more chocolate cake), my dad drove us over to the rink.

As we entered the parking area, I spotted Hank getting off the city bus with Herbie tagging behind him.

"Dad, quick. Beep so Hank and Herbie see us."

Dad made such a loud beep that everyone near us turned around.

"That'll be the last time he beeps for *me*," I thought to myself.

Hank and Herbie ran behind our car and gave Jack a big welcome as he got out of the car. It made me feel really good and Jack seemed pretty happy about it, too.

"Hey, man, whasssup Jack?"

Jack was really busting up and Hank stood there looking at Herbie just shaking his head.

"Herbie, man, do you need help," Hank laughed.

"Come on, son, you're going to be late for your game. It's almost four-thirty and you're not even in your hockey gear yet," said my dad.

My dad and mom are both pretty intense about being on time, no matter what the event is. Even if I am sleeping, I'm sure they are wondering if I'm sleeping on time! Man, what is it about parents!

"Run in and get all your gear on and I'll hang here and make sure Herbie and Hank don't get too wild with Jack," said my dad.

"Maybe Jack wants to come into the locker room with me, Dad. I don't think my coach will mind."

"Are you sure about that son? He can be a mean machine before the game if he thinks his boys aren't serious about what they're doing!"

"Come on, Harry," Hank kicked in. "Get on with your stuff. Herbie and I will show Jack around the rink and especially the snack bar. It's your first game and you're playing one of the toughest teams in the league. You'd better get your head into the game, Harry Jones. Ya know what I mean?"

"Thanks, guys. I'll see you after the game, Jack. Watch these guys around food, they can be like suction cups."

"That's it, Harry Jones. You're asking for it now," yelled Hank as Herbie started chasing me into the locker-room area. I knew Jack would be in good hands and I was kind of excited about him hangin' out with my friends from home. It really made me feel good.

Locker rooms are pretty wild before a game. Either people are really loud or really quiet. Tonight everyone was really quiet because we were up against a really good team, the Falcons. They had one tough goalie. I play defense and I knew the guys who I was up against really were mean machines. If you bumped into any of them it was like hitting a brick wall.

My game started late because the college kids were slow to give up the ice. Their season hadn't officially started, but the way they were hogging the ice you would have thought they were in the middle of a tournament. I shouldn't have dissed them because we don't pay that much for our ice time. They give up a certain amount of time to our league so that young kids like me can have a chance to build their skills early. I always feel really important hangin' around the rink; they treat us kind of special. My dad says they are great "role models" for us. You know, kind of like good examples of people you might want to be like someday.

Finally the game started. Most of the kids on the Falcons team were twice my size and I'm no shortie. They practiced in a rink out in Milton, not too far from Boston. Every single one of them was a star player. Our team, the Jets, is good, but maybe not as good as the Falcons. The joke is, which is faster, a Jet or a Falcon? I guessed we'd find out.

This was really my first big game. I started skating with my cousin when I was about five. Now my cousin wants to be a basketball player, but I really want to stay with hockey. My dad has been a pretty good sport about having to do all the driving now. When my cousin skated, we had a carpool to the rink and it was a lot closer, just down the street. Now that I am on a team, my dad has to drive me to three different places for practice and games. This is the year that you start getting really serious about the game. I'm a pretty tall fourth grader and I am fast on my feet. At least that's what I heard my coach tell my dad.

"Go Jets! Come on, Harry. Watch your backside!"

I could hear Herbie rink-side cheering me on and dissing the Falcons. The Falcons were fast on their feet and our other defense player was not feeling too good, so I was getting a little nervous about what was coming at me. I wanted Jack to see me play a good game, but, hey, this team was tough.

The buzzer sounded and they already had their second goal. I thought our goalie was either asleep or scared. The Falcons were slipping that puck in from the side as fast as lightning. Then I could hear my dad's voice.

"Come on, Jets, get tough. You got plenty of time."

Stand Tall, Harry

By halftime we were down by two and pretty tired. Half my team looked like they were ready to switch to basketball. I think it might have been better if we had started the season with a team that wasn't as good as the Falcons so we could have felt a little better about our playing. Jack looked like he was having a good time, but I kind of wished my team was winning. I looked up into the bleachers during a timeout and Herbie seemed to be keeping everyone happy. From the time he found out I would be playing some of my games at his brother's college rink, he had become the rink know-it-all.

Maybe Hank turned to Henry just for a break from Herbie, who has what Mrs. Lamont would call "undeveloped" listening skills, whatever that means! It sure has been hard for Herbie being the youngest of that big family of boys. Since I've always wanted a brother, I think he's pretty lucky.

The second half of our game was starting to go much better. Steady Eddie, one of our best players, made a goal and I could hear his mom going crazy whooping it up on the side of the rink. Our coach was looking pretty excited. The kid I was covering was like a snake out on the ice and it was hard to know where he would go next. He definitely had a fast sideshot, so I was staying on his outside. He was so big that I was almost against the boards guarding him. My dad always tells me to keep my space from the boards. He worries about an accident, even though he acts like there's no problem out on the ice. I think my mom, being a nurse and all, gives him some bad stories from the hospital. I know that's why she doesn't come to a lot of my games.

I kept hoping for one more goal so we could at least tie the Falcons. Steady Eddie looked dog-tired. The other fast shot on our team, Timmy, had had his tonsils removed and since this was his first time out, the coach was going easy on him. Suddenly, I saw Steady Eddie break down the side of the rink and thread a pass that was intercepted. I saw an opportunity to go on the outside and try for a low shot.

Just as my stick hit the puck and I flicked the low shot, I could hear my dad's voice yelling, "Harry, watch the edge of the boards."

"Harry, Harry. Can you hear me, son. It's Coach Desmond. Harry, open your eyes if you can hear me son."

As I slowly opened my eyes, I had this sensation in my chest that made me feel as if my body was all pain. I could hear someone telling people to move aside. I could feel them moving me off the ice. I just wanted to know if my slideshot made it into the net.

All I remembered about the ride in the ambulance was a man asking me questions. He kept telling me not to close my eyes. As they were wheeling me into the hospital, my mom, dad, and Grampy came over to me, but the man told them he had to hurry. I thought my mom had been crying, but I wasn't sure. My dad kept telling me how great my shot was and that we tied the Falcons. As I began to pass through a set of doors, I saw the words "Emergency Room" written on them so I knew where I was going.

"Careful. Careful now. He hit the boards pretty hard. Let's try to move him onto the table as carefully as we can. He's in a lot of pain. I think we should just cut his jersey. Ask them to put out a page to the person on call in orthopedics. This boy may need to be admitted."

Chapter Eight

"Well, Harry, I see you're finally waking up. I'm Lisa, your nurse, and I have to say you really have everybody around here hopping!"

"Where's my friend?" I asked. "I promised him that we'd go to Herbie's after the game."

"Is your friend's name Jack?"

"Yeah, Jack James. He was at my hockey game with me and then he was going to spend the night."

"Well, he tried to spend the night all right, Harry. I think some of your friends and a big brother finally took him home. That still left half your team here. It was like an ice rink down there in our waiting area. There isn't one snack or drink left in the vending machines. Your friends sure do eat!"

"Where are my parents?" I asked.

"They'll be in as soon as they finish talking to your doctor. You did quite a job on yourself, young man. You must have hit those boards like a ton of bricks."

"Am I gonna be able to go to practice this week?"

Somehow I knew that the answer was going to be something I didn't want to hear. I just ached all over, especially when I took a breath. I was also feeling kind of dizzy. I knew using a hockey stick or getting on a pair of skates was not going to be easy. I wasn't sure I wanted to hear her answer.

"Listen, Harry. I'm no doctor so I think you'd better hold onto your questions for the doctor. He'll be in very soon."

Just as Lisa the nurse was finishing her sentence, my parents came in with the doctor. I could tell by looking at the worry in my mom's face that I wasn't gonna get good news.

"I just hope my season is not finished," I thought to myself.

"Harry, how are you feeling, son?" asked my dad as he put his arm around my mom and brought her closer to my bed. I knew as soon as he did this that trouble was coming.

Whenever my dad has to deliver bad news, he always puts his arm around my mom, but not in a playful way.

"Harry, this is Dr. Roberts. He took care of you last night and he's going to be the doctor taking care of your injuries and your back," said my dad.

My mom freaked as soon as my dad got the word "back" out of his mouth.

"H. P.!"

"Maybe I can help out, Mr. and Mrs. Jones," Dr. Roberts began.

"Harry needs to hear about why he's here and the extent of his injury," he added.

"Harry, I do want you to know that I heard your team tied the Falcons thanks to your low slideshot. I think your team was pretty impressed with how you were able to do all that. Many of them were here until very late last night."

"I already told him there isn't one drink or snack left," piped in Lisa.

"Harry, I think your friends might have eaten Lisa's favorite snack. What do you think?"

When he finished, Lisa shrugged her shoulders, and as she went out the door, she said, "I can tell when I'm not wanted!"

Everyone started to laugh, except me. Nothing seemed very funny.

"Anyway, Harry, I want to tell you about your injuries," said Dr. Roberts. "It took so long to get your CT scan done that we decided to keep you overnight. We were concerned that you had a concussion. You hit the edge of the boards where the wood and the glass meet, at full speed. You do have a clavicle fracture. The clavicle is the S-shaped bone that connects the sternum and the scapula. The scapula kind of connects your muscles. We've wrapped you up pretty tight in a figure-eight bandage. You may be a little uncomfortable for a while. We'll give you some medicine to take home to help with the pain."

Dr. Roberts went on, "Because of the extent of your injuries, they took some X rays last night. The radiologist who read them, Harry, noticed that you may have a mild scoliosis, but it could also be a result of a little painful splinting of the spine due to your injuries. As you begin to heal, we'll take another look. But for now, we'll just monitor it. Since you're looking a little confused, let me at least explain to you what scoliosis means. Scoliosis is a lateral curvature of the spine. It's sort of like this, Harry," and as he explained, he drew a picture on his pad of a healthy spine and one of a spine that showed some curvature.

"I have suggested that once you are more comfortable and the healing process has begun, that your parents make an appointment for you to come in and see me so I can just take another look. I am actually a spine specialist and I got called in last night when you arrived. The scoliosis is not something you need to worry about. As for your injuries, I am going to ask you to follow my rules and be patient. You're a very lucky young man, you know. I was pretty worried when I first took a look at you."

"When can I get back on the ice, Dr. Roberts?" I needed to know right away.

"Harry, your injuries are the kind that need to be babied a bit to be sure that you heal properly. I know this is hard for you to hear, but you may need to sit out the rest of the season. Injuries like yours can be tricky. You may get quite uncomfortable if you put your body in a situation that it isn't ready to handle. Rather than do more damage, you need to be sure that your clavicle not only heals, but heals well. I'm sorry to tell you this, Harry, but I think, for this season, you may not be skating."

I could feel the tears filling my eyes and I could see them in my dad's eyes, too. He loves hockey and it is something that we both like to do. It's our weekend activity and had been since I was old enough to skate. This was my first big game ever and here I was in a hospital bed.

"Go ahead, son, let it out. I don't blame you one bit. This is a tough blow and I know how disappointed you are," said my dad.

I didn't want to cry in front of the doctor, but I could feel the tears running down my cheeks. I was glad when my dad nodded to the doctor, thanked him, and walked over to let him out of the room. As soon as the door shut behind him, my tears started coming out so fast it was like a face flood. The harder I cried, the more my body hurt. Finally, the pain was getting so bad I couldn't bear to cry anymore.

"Harry, right now there is nothing that we can say to you. We all feel your pain and disappointment, but sometimes these things happen in sports, son. We read about it in the paper every day. You'll feel better once you get home. We just need to be patient and see how things heal," said my dad.

I could tell by the way my dad and mom were looking at each other that they were as upset as I was. My dad left the room and pretty soon Lisa, my nurse, came in with a wheel-chair and said I could go home. She was a lot more quiet than before and I could tell that she was feeling bad for me, too.

Just getting into the wheelchair made my body ache. I could tell this was not going to be easy. I began thinking about Hank and Herbie and Jack. I really needed my friends and especial-ly my Grampy. I could hear him saying, "Stand tall, Harry, be proud of who you are."

As we were pulling into our driveway at home, I looked up and saw my coach and Grampy sitting on our front stoop. My coach had the hockey puck and stick from the game and the stick looked like it had writing on it. I bet my whole team had signed the stick, I thought to myself. This made me even sadder. I could tell by the look on my coach's face that he already knew I would be sitting out the season. Just looking at him made me want to cry. All I could think about was not being on the ice.

My Grampy saw the tears start to roll again and quickly came to my rescue.

"Coach, Harry is not feeling like himself, but I know he appreciates your being here and bringing the stick and all."

As my eyes met my coach's, the tears were coming down even faster. I hated having him see me cry.

The words "thanks, coach" felt like they were stuck to my lips. I just wasn't ready to see anybody yet. All I could think of was my bed.

"Come on, Harry. I think you and your Grampy have things to do," and I could see Grampy motioning to my mom and dad to stay behind. There were times when my mom just seemed to know that Grampy had a better idea. This was one of them.

Grampy had my bed all ready and had moved it so that I could get in and out by supporting myself on a side table. He had everything all set and had even made me some rice and peas and homemade cornbread. This is one of my favorite meals and nobody makes it like my Grampy. At first I didn't want to eat, but it smelled so good that I finally gave in.

Trying to eat when I could hardly sit up was very difficult. The food seemed to go everywhere. Grampy watched me but never asked one question or said one word to me. I couldn't remember a time when he had been so quiet.

When my mom and dad came in, Grampy sent them off and told my mom he had my room all set. I could see her checking it out.

"You're good, Dad," she said as she walked past him. "The hospital can always use a fine nurse like you."

She continued, "Harry, if you need me I will be in my bedroom. I think your Grampy wants to give me the day off."

My dad, who still looked pretty upset, nodded to me and followed behind my mom.

After I finished eating, and I was a lot more hungry than I thought, my Grampy helped me get into bed. I just wanted to zone out for a while and have some time alone. I was a little worried about school and nothing seemed right anymore; if you know what I mean. Suddenly, it was as if my Grampy had moved into my head and knew everything I was thinking.

"Harry, we're gonna talk about all this later, but I don't want you worrying about school. Our people are strong and they have always stood proud, no matter what. You just stand tall, Harry, stand tall and it will all work out. I promise. As long as I have stood tall, I have made it through a lot of hard times, so I know you can do the same."

"Harry, are you sleeping again?" and as I began to open my eyes I saw Jack standing next to me with a big smile on his face and a box all wrapped up with blue paper.

"Harry, this is for you. My dad and I picked it out for you and we think it is something that you might enjoy and me, too."

I was having trouble unwrapping it, but finally managed. I was glad Jack didn't take it back and do it for me. I was so happy to see him.

"Oh, wow, it's a portable chess set! I have always wanted my very own set. Jack, this is awesome. Thank you so much!"

"Harry, the pieces have magnets on them to help you so they don't slip and my dad says they are all hand-carved."

"Next to hockey, chess is the game I love the most," I said. "I just can't believe I have my very own chess set. Jack, I can't believe this is mine." I kept mumbling this over and over again. Jack just sat there with a big Cheshire-cat smile all over his face.

"Did you hear I can't play hockey this season? And on top of that, my back isn't straight, either."

Poor Jack couldn't get a word in. I just let it all pour out.

"Harry, remember? I saw it all happen and I have to tell you I was pretty scared that you weren't gonna be okay. Hank and Herbie stayed with me while your dad ran down to the ice. I got this really weird feeling when the ambulance came. Herbie's older brother and some of the guys on his hockey team came over and took care of all of us. It was almost as bad as when my first rabbit died. Herbie's older brother and his friends were so amazing. They made me feel so welcome. Of course, Herbie insisted we stay until almost the end of the game, which Hank said was odd because Herbie hates hockey. After the game, they even brought me into the locker room so I could see it. Then Herbie's brother took us all over to the hospital and we sat with your mom and dad for a while. Almost your whole team came over with us.

"Then they gave me a ride home, but I think Herbie's brother thought I lived in another state. He was so funny. He kept saying, 'Jack, my man, what are they doing making you live way out here? This is like the days when there weren't any cities.' Then, just when he thought we had completely left what he called 'civilization,' he spotted a Dunkin' Donuts and just about took a nutty. Harry, it was one of the funniest things I have ever seen," said Jack.

Chapter Eight

"By this time it was pretty late and so we decided to stop at the Dunkin' Donuts and call my parents. There aren't any streetlights out there like there are here and Herbie's brother kept saying 'It sure is black out here.' He reminded me of Bill Cosby. He was so funny, Harry. Even Herbie and Hank started in with him and it helped to take my mind off of you."

Jack continued, "While we waited for my parents to come, we each got a donut and some hot chocolate. It was the latest I had ever been to a Dunkin' Donuts. We were just finishing up when my parents got there. They asked Herbie's brother and everyone if they wanted to come to the house for a bit, but it was pretty late and Herbie's brother had to get his parents' car back. My dad helped him get out to the main roads even though he said he didn't need help. Harry, I really like your friends. I was pretty upset about your accident, but I did have a really fun ride home."

"Harry, how's the hockey star?" It was Jack's dad poking his head in my room and I could see his mom standing behind his dad.

"Hi, Mr. and Mrs. James. Thank you so much for the chess set. It's awesome and I think I'll be using it a lot. I don't think I'm going to be able to play hockey the rest of the season, but I'm not sure yet."

"Harry, that's a tough break," said Jack's dad. "I remember breaking my leg skiing on my first day and sitting out all season. My sister and brother continued to ski, so it was a long time for me. That's how I learned to play chess. My dad, who wasn't really into skiing that much, used to hang back with me and we'd play together."

Jack's parents always made me feel so good and it was easy to talk to them. When I first woke up and saw Jack, I wasn't sure I was ready to deal with anyone, but then I was really glad he had come.

"Harry, are you with us? It looks like you're dozing off again." My mom, always the nurse.

"Harry, we actually need to get going and you need your rest. You and Jack can get together next week. We just needed to see that you were okay and let you know we are always thinking of you," said Jack's mom.

I could tell that Jack really wanted to stay, but his mom and dad had other ideas. Even after my mom insisted on giving them some tea or coffee, they said no. I think I started to doze off so I wasn't sure when they left.

Chapter Nine

*I wanted to know everything my dad could
tell me about these chess tournaments.*

"Harry, while I pull the car out, you gather up your things.
Grampy will carry them out for you. I know we're
going to hit a lot of traffic getting out of the city."

My mom had decided to drive me to school, which she
almost never did. She needed to check in with the school
nurse and with Mrs. Lamont. I kind of wanted to take the bus
and see Jeb, but when I thought about that long, long ride to
school, I knew that getting a lift from my mom would be a
zillion times better. I knew she would talk to Mrs. Lamont
about my hockey game and I sure didn't want to do that
myself. All the kids would just sit there looking at me the way
we look at everybody who has somethin' special goin' on.

Grampy walked me out and I could tell he wanted to come,
too, but my mom had her own way of letting him know that

she needed to do this alone. As he helped me into the car with all my stuff, he whispered in my ear, " *Stand tall, Harry,* and have a good day. Everything is gonna be fine."

Even though I was still not feeling very comfortable, the ride out to my school was really easy. My mom took roads that the bus can't take. We even made a stop at Dunkin' Donuts, which reminded me of Jack's story about Herbie's brother. I saw two of the teachers from my school in there getting coffee and each of them stopped by the car and said hi.

Going into the office to see the nurse was kind of strange at the beginning of school. The office was full and everybody seemed to have a special story. I was glad when the nurse told my mom to take me to class first and then come back.

As we started down the hall, I could hear Tommy behind me talking to someone. All of a sudden he was in front of us asking me how come my mom was with me. He was really concerned and it made me feel good. While I was explaining the game to him, Mrs. Lamont came out in the hall and met us. She asked Tommy to move on into class.

I was really worried about school and sitting because I was still very sore, and it kind of ached when I moved in a certain way. Mrs. Lamont asked Jack if he wanted to be my writing buddy, which was awesome. She said he could help me with anything I needed help with and that each day she and I would talk about how things were going. She asked me if I had anything to do during recess and gym and I told her I had a new chess set. She said that I could use the picnic table outside during recess and that in gym I could read, play chess, or relax in the nurse's office.

Going into my classroom was not as weird as I thought it would be at all. Everyone was so ready to help me that it was almost too much. There were so many extra hands. I finally knew how an octopus must feel. What a confusing life it must have!

Mrs. Lamont came up to me when my mom left and asked me if I felt comfortable talking about my accident. A lot of the kids were asking me about how it happened and I was getting tired of saying the same thing over and over. Mrs. Lamont said that if I told everybody together it might be easier. I told her I wasn't sure I wanted to. She said she would help me out and we could just talk about it a little.

We usually start each Monday with our sharing. We always sit in a circle on the rug and Mrs. Lamont begins by sharing her weekend, which sometimes seems really boring, except for her stories about her dog. Grampy would call that dog a little devil, for sure. I had so much help getting on the rug that I thought they were going to sit me down, too. After Mrs. Lamont finished about her weekend, in this loud voice Tommy called out, "Let Harry go next!" Mrs. Lamont was very calm about it all and looked over at Tommy in a way that made him quiet again and we could hear this little "sorry." Jack volunteered to go next, which really helped me out. When he told the story about Herbie's brother and the drive out here, everyone laughed, even Mrs. Lamont.

After Jack finished, Mrs. Lamont looked over at me and asked me if I wanted to add anything. At first I was going to say no, but the look on Tommy's face made me share just a little. It was my classmates who figured out how hard it was for me not to be able to play hockey anymore this year. I didn't even have to tell them myself. They made me understand that they really got it, but I was starting to feel a little sad. Just when I thought that I might cry, Mrs. Lamont asked if there were any chess players in the group besides Jack and me. Only one other hand went up and then Tommy raised his as a "wannabe chess player" and everyone laughed.

Mrs. Lamont is such a caring teacher. She always knows when it is time to move on or to make someone feel better. I'm having the best year in school I have ever had and my mom and dad say that a lot of it is Mrs. Lamont and the other part is Jack. I think they are right about both things.

My school day went all right. I played a lot of great chess during my free times and the kids were great. When I was waiting for the bus, Mrs. Harrington, the coordinator for the Boston program, sat down and played out some of Jack's game with me. While she was sitting there, she told me that they had tournaments kids could play in. I told her about the story in our

Stand Tall, Harry

Scholastic News and the International Chess Tournament. I was thinking to myself that when I got home I might want to look for the newspaper and read the article again.

Jeb wasn't on the bus going home, which made me kind of sad. The other kids helped me out and Mr. Barrett was great. He even told me I could fall asleep if I wanted and he'd wake me up when we got to my stop. I was feeling pretty tired.

I think my eyes started drooping as soon as we pulled out of the school parking lot. I guess that by the time we got to the Dunkin' Donuts area, I was sound asleep. I dreamed I was playing in a chess tournament and that my whole class was there cheering me on. Just as I was about to find out if I won, Mr. Barrett was standing there tapping my head and saying, "Okay, son, time to get off. Your Grampy is here waiting for you."

I couldn't wait to get home and set up my chess set. Grampy always gives me some free time before I start my homework and all I wanted to do with that time was play chess. I was still pretty sore and so I thought I'd lie on my bed or on the couch and play. Since my board is magnetic, I could play just about anywhere.

Whenever you play a game of chess with my Grampy, you learn about more than just chess. He is an awesome chess player and he always begins each game by looking up to the heavens and saying, "Pop, I want you to know we're playing that game again and I'm thinking of you."

My Grampy learned how to play chess from his father, who had to make his own chess pieces out of sticks he found in the woods. Life was very hard in those days. People weren't very nice to people of color and so our folks didn't have much of anything. And if anyone saw them enjoying what they did have, they'd come around and break it up and not get punished.

"You're lucky, Harry," said Grampy. "Today, people are worrying less about the outside of a person and more about what's inside. That's all that really counts, Harry. Always remember that."

By the time my dad came home, I had Grampy's king trapped and Grampy didn't look one bit happy.

Chapter Nine

"Who taught you how to play this game anyway, Harry? My army is feeling pretty bad right now."

Sometimes I wondered if Grampy was playing as hard as he could because it was me he was playing. My dad is a different story. He hates losing a game to anyone, especially someone as young as me. Those are serious chess games.

At dinner, I told my dad about the dream I had on the bus about being in a chess tournament and I also told him what Mrs. Harrington said. I thought my dad would laugh, but instead he got real interested and he told me about some friends at his job who play in tournaments every weekend they can. I guess there's a web site that tells you when the tournaments are. My dad said that you can sign up on the web to play and that there should be some tournaments that do not cost too much money.

Usually our school-night dinners are kind of quick, but this meal ended up being kind of long. I wanted to know everything my dad could tell me about the chess tournaments. I started thinking about the *Scholastic News* story I had read about the kid who was a world-famous International Master. I remembered the story saying that some chess group had paid for a lot of his trip to this big tournament that was really far away. I was pretty sure the article was still in my desk at school.

"Harry, we are going to be in big trouble with your mama if you don't get started on your homework," said Grampy. "It's almost seven o'clock, son. H. P. Junior, you go get Harry organized and I'll clean up."

My Grampy is like the camp director in our house when my mom isn't around. My dad will always kid around with him, and say, "Okay, boss, consider it done!" Even though Grampy isn't his dad, he is like a dad to him. Grampy is nuts over my sister, Consuela, too. Consuela was a little girl when my parents married and Grampy became her best buddy, just like he is to me.

As I was finishing my homework and dreaming of my nice, comfortable bed, my mom called to remind my dad I had to have a sponge bath. When my dad hung up, he looked over at me with a twinkle in his eye and said, "You're gonna wish I had just let that phone ring, Harry."

Just as he finished his sentence, Grampy called up and asked, "Need any help getting Harry washed? Don't forget to be real careful!"

My dad whispered under his breath, "That is Mama II talking to me because he doesn't even know that Mama I just called."

Then we both started laughing.

Getting washed was a drag, but we did it. I felt that only part of my body was clean. I hadn't been thinking about hockey all day, but in bed I kept wondering why I ever went for that shot the way I did. I just couldn't believe I might be out of hockey for the rest of the year. Bummer!

Chapter Ten

"**H**arry Jones, rise and shine boy or you're gonna be running after that school bus!"

"Can't I just stay in bed five more minutes, Mom? Come on, I'm injured."

"No way, Harry. I can't drive you to school today. Since I have to bring you to Dr. Roberts this afternoon, I had to reorganize my schedule."

"Dr. Roberts, already," I yelled. "Mom, what is he going to do to me today? It is really gonna hurt, 'cause I'm sore, Mom, really sore."

"Harry Jones. You just relax, boy. I'm not just your mother, I'm a nurse, too. Do you think I would let him hurt you? You want to be able to swing a hockey stick again, don't you?"

"Well, yeah, but."

"No buts about it. Now let's get you up and off on time."

I can always tell when my mom means business. I put myself in high gear and moved along.

Just as I got to the bus stop, Mr. Barrett was coming around the bend and I could see Jeb sitting in the frontseat talking to him. As soon as the bus stopped, Jeb jumped out and grabbed my backpack, asking me all about how I was feeling. When I got on the bus everybody yelled, "Harry, whasssup, man!" It sounded pretty funny hearing this come out of the mouths of kindergartners, too. I burst out laughing and I could tell that Jeb had put some practice time into this.

Normally, Jeb and I sit in the back of the bus, but today I was glad we were staying in the front. Besides, Mr. Barrett was enjoying our talk and I kept seeing this big grin come on his face. I told Jeb all about the game and how I hit the boards. He had already heard about some of it from a friend of Herbie's brother. People think of Boston as huge, but news gets around just as fast as it does in the country. When I try to tell that to my friends at school, they just raise their eyebrows, all except Jack. Now that he's come to visit, he knows that my neighborhood is not a lot different from his except that I'm in the city.

The ride went really fast and I couldn't believe it when Mr. Barrett drove into the school parking lot. Jeb offered to help me and Mr. Barrett even said he'd wait. I didn't have to carry my backpack, which really helped a lot.

Mrs. Lamont had sent Tommy to the cafeteria to meet me. Jack had told me that he had a dentist appointment and would be coming in late. On the way to class, Tommy asked if I had my new chess set with me.

"I think he wants to learn how to play," I thought to myself.

I didn't mind teaching him, but I also wanted to play with Jack if he came in before recess.

"Tommy, how about this," I explained. "If Jack isn't back by recess, I'll show you a little about the game. But if he's back, you can just watch us play and I promise to teach you another time. By the way, my mom packed a few extra chocolate chip cookies today so I'll share them with you."

"Oh, thanks, Harry, but I don't want to take your cookies. Your mom gave them to you to eat."

I was sure Tommy really wanted the cookies, but he was holding back. I brought the extras to share with him and I really hoped he'd change his mind. Just when I was about to say this to him, Mrs. Lamont made us all sit down for morning exercises.

Jack came in just before recess and I could see that Tommy was bummed about me not teaching him how to play chess during recess. I told him he could watch and maybe learn that way, but I knew that would be hard. Jack and I don't like to talk when we play. We kind of do a lot of thinking but no talking.

Jack really had me cornered when the whistle blew for us to pack up and go in. Just when I thought it was over, I made a really good move and won the game. Jack went nuts and Tommy started laughing really hard, which really annoyed Jack. Sometimes Tommy laughs at the wrong time. This was one of those times, but Tommy just didn't get it.

Chapter Ten

Gym came right after recess and Mrs. Lamont told me I could bring my chess set if I wanted since the kids were going to go through an obstacle course. Jack really loved gym so he went right out there, but Tommy didn't look too happy about it. I noticed him holding his stomach and talking to our gym teacher. A few minutes later he came over and sat with me. I figured out right away that this was going to give him time to learn how to play chess. I wasn't sure if I was happy about it because of the way he had laughed at Jack, but Grampy says not to judge everyone and to try and help them along. Grampy and I have lots of "Tommy talks." I told Tommy to sit very quietly and not to laugh or our gym teacher might make him go back in.

"Okay, Tommy," I began. "Now I want you to listen really carefully to everything I say. Chess has white pieces and black pieces or sometimes they can be other colors, but Grampy says real chess has only white and black, kind of like checkers has black and red. This is how you set up the board. Make sure the kings and queens from each team are facing each other. You put the white queen on a white square and the black queen on a black square. White always gets to make their move first. For now, just remember that only one piece gets to move at a turn. The knight, this guy here that looks like a horse's head, is the only piece that gets to jump over the other pieces."

Just as I finished, our gym teacher came over. I thought he was going to scold Tommy, but instead he asked him if he needed to see the nurse. Tommy told him he would be okay if he could just sit quietly.

"Well, maybe Harry will brush you up on a few chess moves while you're resting," our gym teacher added as he walked away.

Tommy started to give out a huge belly laugh until I told him to stop.

"A belly laugh like that doesn't happen if you're sick, Tommy. Do ya think?"

"I guess not, Harry," Tommy whined.

"You know, Tommy. You don't always pick a good time to laugh, like today when Jack lost the game. He was kind of annoyed at you and I don't think you even knew it. Nobody is happy about losing and when you laugh at them, it can hurt their feelings. Some kids even get mad at that. Do ya know what I mean, Tommy?"

At first I thought I had hurt his feelings and I felt bad, but then he looked up and said, "I know you're right, Harry, but sometimes it just comes out."

"Well, Tommy, my Grampy says that if you know it's coming, try to watch for it."

We both kind of giggled and I went back to explaining the game. I heard our gym teacher blow the whistle and decided to pack up.

"Tommy, I promise to teach you more another time. Okay?"

"No problem, Harry. I can't afford one of these sets, anyway, so it's okay if we don't finish."

I could tell Tommy was starting to get down on himself again. He did this a lot and I always felt bad. He really is a good kid, but I don't think he knows it.

"Now listen, Tommy. If I don't finish teaching you, you're only going to be able to play part of a chess game and that's pretty weird. I promise, we will finish this lesson sometime soon and then I'll even play a game with you. Deal?"

"Deal, Harry," Tommy answered with a half-surprised smile on his face.

I was starting to get into a new routine in school and it was feeling more and more okay. I was getting really hot about chess and today, when Jack got to school just in time for recess, I told him about my chess dream on the bus and how excited my Grampy had been when he heard about it.

"Even my dad is getting into it, Jack. You know, Jack, the one thing my dad loves more than his computer is hockey and the one thing he loves more than hockey is chess."

Jack looked over at me with this big grin on his face.

"Harry, that sounds like my dad, but for him, first it's his computer, then basketball, and then chess. No wonder we're such good friends."

Jack and I walked in from lunch recess really cracking up about how much alike we are.

Chapter Ten

The afternoons in school kind of dragged. I would get a little uncomfortable even though Mrs. Lamont had given me a soft chair to sit in. I stopped the pain medication because it was making me too sleepy. I was just taking stuff that you don't need a prescription for. My mom was in charge and in school the nurse took care of everything. Even so, my body still didn't feel like things were gettin' better.

Sometimes I would start worrying about my "back" appointment. But first I had to heal. My mom had scheduled my "back" appointment for the same day as one of my other doctor's appointments because it's all part of the same department at the hospital. Even though she kept telling me scoliosis is just a curvature of the spine and not to worry, I was very worried. I know someone in school with it and she wears a brace. I see her sometimes in the nurse's office when she comes in to take the brace off for gym class. It looks like a piece of armor. I kept thinking to myself, "Maybe they only give them to girls and not to boys."

My sister, Consuela, would really get on me for that one. She says that girls can do anything boys can do, so I sure won't share this idea with her!

One good thing about being in my school with a sore body was that Mrs. Lamont let me have a jump-start on the end of the day. I was allowed to pick a buddy and leave my class five minutes early for the bus. Jack would get this big grin on his face about two-fifteen and I could tell he had checked out and was ready to help me pack up. Mrs. Lamont was always two steps ahead of us. She'd look over at Jack and say, "Jack, I hope you are reading your book and not that clock up there."

"Yes, Mrs. Lamont. I'm still reading," Jack would reply.

Then Mrs. Lamont would get that funny little twinkle in her eye that kind of said, "Oh sure, Jack, you are reading all right." Nothing ever gets by her. My Grampy has an expression, "Sharp as a tack," and that's our Mrs. Lamont. The kids call her "radar." One thing for sure is that she makes school seem like an adventure and it makes me really want to do my work and learn about things I never liked before.

On the way home from school, Jeb was on the bus and we got a chance to really hash out all the stuff that was going on.

When I told him about my new chessboard, I found out that his grandfather played, too, but no one had taught Jeb how. Our bus ride home ended up being a chess lesson, but we didn't get much farther than I had gotten with Tommy. We didn't take the game out until we were halfway home.

When the bus pulled up to my corner, I saw my mom waiting in the car for me with the engine running.

"Mom, Mom. What are you doin' comin' to my bus stop?" I thought to myself.

I was afraid that Mr. Barrett would say something more, maybe about my back, so I did a quick cover and said, "Have to run, Jeb, or I'll be late for my doctor's appointment. That's my mom waiting in the car right there."

"Jeb," said Mr. Barrett. "You help Harry out with his bag and come right back so I'm not late finishing up my route."

Mr. Barrett probably knew Jeb would help me, anyway, but he was always lettin' us know who was the bus "boss man."

Jeb got up and went down the stairs in front of me. I was hoping my mom *really* was going right to the doctor's appointment and that she wouldn't say anything else to Jeb. Who wants their mother at the bus stop anyway?

"Hi, Mrs. Jones. I'm Jeb Burns. Here's Harry's bag."

"Nice to meet you, Jeb. Thank you for helping Harry. I'm sorry, but we have to get going to Harry's appointment. We'll chat another time. It's nice to meet you, Jeb. Harry enjoys riding out to school with you."

I felt this huge cloud move from over my head. I slid into the car and off we went.

Chapter Eleven

*After I had a quick snack, Grampy and I
sat down and started a game of chess.*

Going to see Dr. Roberts again was not so bad. He said basketball was his sport and that he knew more about hockey injuries than the sport. Dr. Roberts is a big Boston Celtics fan so it was fun to hear him talk a little about basketball. He was surprised that I knew so many of the old Celtics players who are in the Hall of Fame. I have my dad to thank for that. For his birthday every year we go to a Celtics game, even though he loves hockey. My dad couldn't play ice hockey when he was little because he lived on an island in the Pacific and there was no ice. He and his friends used to play basketball.

My appointment didn't take that long and on the way home, my mom drove by this hall where she said they play chess every Saturday. I had a feeling that she and my dad were talking a lot about my chess and I saw my Grampy actin' kind of excited whenever I played. It seemed like he and my dad might have been reading up on chess tournaments because they knew a lot more than they ever said before. Each day after school someone had time to play chess with me between my homework and dinner. Even after dinner sometimes, my dad and I might start a game. I didn't watch TV for over a week, but I've never been allowed to watch it a lot anyway. Grampy and dad were becoming the chess nerds!

When I got home from my doctor's appointment, my Grampy said that Jack had called to see how I did. It was a long distance call for him so it was really special. I couldn't remember a time when one of my school friends had called me at home. I was pretty excited and Mom said that I could call him back if I only talked for a few minutes. Since Jack and I both have E-mail, I didn't mind making it short. I was just excited that he had called.

I told Jack all about the appointment and he said that his dad called him from work and told him about this chess tournament for new "competitors" that was going to be in a city outside of Boston. It cost $12 to play and your parents could register and pay for you over the Internet. In fact, I think that I pass a sign for the city where it's happening each day on my way to school. Jack said his dad would print the application and the name of the web site and give it to Jack to bring to me at school. Jack said that he might enter it, too. Since I was used to playing Jack, I was pretty excited about that, but I wasn't sure if Jack and I would be allowed to play a tournament game against each other.

When I got off the phone, my dad was coming in the door from work and my mom was going out the door to go to her work. My dad asked me how my doctor's appointment was and then I saw him showing something to my mom. He seemed very excited.

While my dad and my Grampy worked on dinner, I did my homework. I could hear them whispering in the kitchen like they had some big secret. I wanted to tell my dad about the chess tournament that Jack told me about, but I didn't have a chance. I was also having trouble doing my math homework

Chapter Eleven

because all I kept thinking about was chess. Finally I finished my work and my dad said he would check it after dinner.

When I went into the kitchen, I could see some papers next to my plate. My dad and my Grampy were looking like they were up to something. I went over and picked them up and written on the top of the paper was "Youth Chess Tournament." As soon as I read it, I started to laugh, and my dad and Grampy thought I had really lost it. Then I started telling them the story of how Jack told me over the phone that his dad had found the same web site.

"Jack says he might want to compete, too," I said excitedly. "The tournament is about halfway between Boston and his town, he said. Besides, I think I'll feel better if someone I know is playing."

"Well, that makes sense, Harry," said my dad. "I'll talk to Jack's dad and we can work out the details. I'm not sure how they choose opponents. I guess we will find out when we get there. I'll go back on the Internet tonight and give them my credit card to get you registered. Since we won't be paying for ice time for a while, we can use the money we put aside for hockey for chess. Your coach says he wants to give back some of the money we paid for the ice time. I told him it's not necessary, but he says he wants to."

I felt kind of bad when my dad said that, and my Grampy started reading my mind again and said, "Stand tall, Harry Jones. I know you miss hockey but you might be a future chess star."

After dinner I had to go right to my reading since the meal had taken longer than usual. There wouldn't be any time for chess. Anyway, I was starting to ache a little and I knew the much-hated sponge bath was coming.

When I finally got into bed, I was so tired that I fell right to sleep. I was in the middle of an awesome chess game when I heard my mom's voice.

"Harry Jones. Do you think you are retired or something? Get out of that bed son and move on into the bathroom. If you don't hurry up you're going to be wearing your pajamas to school."

"Yeah. They'll think you are going to a slumber party!" my dad yelled out.

I could hear my dad and my Grampy cracking up in the kitchen. What a pair those two made. Sometimes it was as if my Grampy always lived upstairs with us. I'm not sure why he even kept his apartment.

The rest of my school week went pretty fast. Jeb, who is not a chess player yet (!), had to listen to my chess updates, kind of like a daily sports report. By the end of the week I was pretty sure Jeb was happy for a break from me and my chess. He's a big basketball fan, so sometimes he talks about basketball the way I talk about chess. The only problem was that I kind of thought I hadn't given him a chance to talk about anything for a while. I had been doing all the talking! I think I was the one who was really becoming the chess nerd. All I did was play chess nearly every free moment I had.

Once I got to school, Jack and I really went into our chess talk. He got a copy of this chess magazine for kids called *School Mates* and we spent our recess reading about all the youth chess tournaments. The magazine is for kids in our age group and there was even an article about some really young kid winning the National Elementary Chess Tournament. Jack told me I could borrow the magazine and give it back to him on Saturday at the tournament. I couldn't wait to show my dad.

Gym was right after lunch on Friday. Tommy pretended he was sick from lunch. We had a substitute gym teacher who said, "Well, you can go to the nurse if you want."

Tommy looked at her with this pained look on his face and said, "I think I just need to sit out on the side and see if I feel any better. If I start feeling like I'm going to vomit, I'll go right to the nurse."

"What a pro this kid is," I thought to myself. I would never have the nerve to do this twice in a row. Right after Tommy came out, Susan went over and said something to the "sub." For a minute I thought maybe she was getting even for Tommy moving her snack into my bag. I think she just asked to go to the bathroom though, because she left the gym for a few minutes and then came back. Tommy looked pretty relieved when she went back into the game. I know he was thinkin' the same thing I was.

Tommy remembered everything I had shown him. I set up the board and we got right into a game. At first he tried to talk to me while we were playing. I gave him very short answers and finally he could see that chess was a game that made you really use what my dad calls "higher-level thinking skills." The moves don't jump right out at you. You really have to think about them for a long time. Chess is not a game that you play if you're a big talker or in a hurry.

Tommy was kind of in a rush, but he was beginning to slow down a little. Of course I could beat him, but I wanted Tommy to feel how great it is to win. I decided to make some silly mistakes and move the game along. Finally, he got the idea and when he said "checkmate," he practically jumped out of his skin. Just when he was about to let out one of his "whoops," I warned him that our principal was standing in the doorway. Tommy quickly got the hint and kept his excitement "in check."

I read *School Mates* on the bus ride home. By the time Mr. Barrett was rounding the corner to my stop, I had read the magazine "from cover to cover." I was getting very excited about the competition and I was also very nervous since I was still not feeling all that comfortable physically yet.

After I had a quick snack, Grampy and I sat down and started a game of chess. I could tell he had waited all day for this. He never got a chance to do things like this after school when he was young. He began working when he was about ten years old. Sometimes I think about that because I am about that age and I don't know what it would be like if I had to work during all my free time.

You know, there are still children today who are forced to work. They live in places far away from us. My dad read an article to me from the newspaper about some friends of his who went over to a place called the Sudan, which is in Africa, and bought the women and children there out of slavery. For $33 each they were able to free all these women and children. That would be like buying my mom and me back. My dad and my Grampy had tears running down their cheeks as my dad was reading the article. My dad has a lot of friends from church who are part of something called the American Anti-Slavery Group and they work to make sure no one ever has to be a slave again.

Last year in school we studied Dr. Martin Luther King, a great man who was killed trying to help everyone get treated the same. I knew a little about him but I didn't know everything. That's the thing. The kids in my school always think I know all about the famous Black people because I'm Black and I want to say to them, "Hey, there's a lot you don't know about famous White people so why would it be any different for me?"

Grampy and I were just getting into our chess game when the doorbell rang. I knew it was Herbie and Hank because they didn't even wait for Grampy to let them in.

"Harry, whassup my man?" and with that they both broke up.

Grampy, who can be very funny sometimes, answered, "Unless your eyes are playing tricks on you boys, chesssss . . . isssss . . . up, that's whasssssup!"

We all started laughing. While Grampy and I gave Hank a chess lesson, Herbie had a piece of my mom's fudge cake. I think he had two because he was in the kitchen a long time. Hank and I don't have to fight off a bunch of brothers for our snacks, so it's a little different for us.

I hadn't gotten a chance to tell Hank and Herbie about the chess tournament.

"Harry, how are you feelin'?" Hank asked.

Before I got to answer, Grampy said, "Well, this boy is doing so well that he's going to be in his first chess tournament tomorrow."

"Whoa! Run that by me again," Herbie yelled out.

"It's true. I am going out to Framingham to play in a chess tournament and Jack is going to play, too."

"You mean like those chess nerds that I read about in school?" Herbie asked.

I started to crack up because he reminded me so much of Tommy that day we came in from recess and he saw the *Scholastic News* article.

"Yeah, that's right, Herbie. So I guess you read the article in your class, too. I saved mine and it's still in my bedroom somewhere."

"Are you doing this 'cause you want to go on a big trip somewhere?" Herbie asked.

Hank started laughing.

"Herbie, why do you ask questions like that?"

Hank and Herbie could be very funny together. I was so happy they were back on track again.

Herbie just didn't give up. "So wait a minute, Harry. Let me get this right. You're gonna sit in a room with a bunch of people tomorrow and play chess?"

"Yeah. Why not? I played hockey in front of a bunch of people!"

"Well, yeah, but . . ."

Before Herbie could finish, Hank had him by the arm and was dragging him out to the hallway and then out the door.

"Time for us to go, Harry. We'll be over tomorrow for an update on how things went. You might be famous if you win, Harry, and then we can say we're your buddies."

Hank is such a great friend. He has always cheered me and Herbie on no matter what we're doing. He'll also tell us if we're being jerks. My mom and dad always say, "He has a good head on his shoulders." Herbie does, too. It just takes him a while to get off of himself. Having all those older brothers has been a trip for him, even though we all know he can't live without them.

Grampy and I played chess for quite a while and then my dad took over for my Grampy. My mom had split her shift again so she could come home for dinner and then return to the hospital for the late shift. My dad drove her because he says that it isn't safe to be walking around so late at night. He says that no matter where you live, things are different now. My Grampy gives the exact same speech!

I decided not to stay up too late since the chess competition was in the morning and we'd all have to get up early to get all the Saturday chores done. My mom and dad have a real system for all that and I have my own chores, but I got to pass on them for a while because of my hockey accident.

Jack called me around seven-thirty. I could tell he hadn't slept very much and he seemed nervous about the tournament. I think I was, too. I had a feeling we wouldn't be able to be opponents. We were going to meet there at eight-thirty and the tournament would begin at nine o'clock. We would have some downtime together.

Chapter Twelve

The drive out to Framingham for the chess tournament was kind of long. The whole family came. Grampy sat in the backseat with me and reported on how many post offices were in each town that we passed. Even though he retired, my mom says that he may as well still be working for the Postal Service. He follows everything they do: new stamps, special services, everything.

All of a sudden my dad pointed out the hotel where the tournament was to take place. It was right before the exit and it looked like a big castle. I was getting so excited. Parts of the hotel looked like giant rooks, which are chess pieces.

"Well, Harry. I can see why they hold the tournaments here, can't you?" my dad said with a little laugh.

My Grampy was next. "Look here. I have seen this place in the travel section of the newspaper. Now I can say I've been here."

We pulled into the parking lot and I spotted Jack's car parked way over on the side, far away from any other cars. Jack said his dad always parks this way. I started to laugh at how the sun was making all those stickers on the back window shine.

When we got inside, there was a sign telling us where to go. I could feel that my parents were as excited as I was. Even though my mom is not really into chess, I knew she and Mrs. James would find plenty to talk about. I could hear Jack calling out my name as my dad checked me in.

"Harry, I'm over here," called out Jack, waving his arms in the air.

My dad looked up and motioned to me where the voice was coming from.

"Harry, first let's make sure they processed your entry and then we'll go over to Jack."

While my dad and I finished up, my mom headed over to Jack, with my Grampy trailing behind. I could tell Grampy couldn't decide whether to wait with my dad and me or go with my mom. So he was kind of in the middle of both!

By the time I got to Jack, his parents were there, too. His father told us that when we went into the tournament room, there would be no talking allowed, which made sense. My mom and Mrs. James decided to hang out in the lobby area, where they had coffee and snacks set up. Jack and I and our dads and my Grampy went into the tournament room just before the tournament started.

When I first sat down, I felt like I was back in the dream I had that day on the bus. I couldn't believe I was there. The chessboards and the whole setup were so amazing. I had never seen so many chessboards and players in one place. The setups were all exactly the same and there was a number next to each board. Jack looked over at me and pointed at them and I knew we were both thinking the same thing.

The boy and the girl playing closest to our seats were even younger than the two of us. When I heard the boy say something to the girl, I could hardly understand him. She just looked at him and then he repeated what he had said and she nodded. Pretty soon a flag went down and their game was over. They had played four five-minute games and she had won three of them.

It was nine o'clock and time for the tournament to start. Someone came over and helped Jack and me to our boards and asked if we had any questions. We would each play three games, whether we won or lost. If we won, we would play the winners the following round. If we lost, we would play the losers. I was feeling a little uncomfortable in the hard chairs. My dad went over as they were setting me up and pretty soon someone came in with a more comfortable chair. I couldn't believe my dad had done this. It made me feel like some wimpy kid! I already stood out a bit because I was the only African-American player in this whole big room and now my dad went and asked for a special chair for me. Unreal!

My opponent ended up being the person who had won the game we had watched and Jack's opponent was someone who had also won a game. His ended up being a boy and mine a girl.

I was kind of nervous about all the people who could wander in and watch us play. Jack kept rolling his eyes, so I thought he was pretty nervous, too, or else he was wondering what he was doing there.

In the beginning of my game I did a stupid thing. I let go of my chess piece to scratch my nose without saying "j'adoube," which is tournament talk and means "I adjust." My opponent got the advantage of my mistake. I had read on the Internet that playing in a tournament is different from other games and you need to remember all the ins and outs.

My first opponent was very good. She never took her eyes off the chessboard. My first game was definitely taking a long time. Just when I was sure she was going to be the winner, she made a silly move and I ended up winning. The same thing happened with my opponent in the next round, but then I lost the third. I ended up winning two games and losing one. I was so excited I could hardly keep quiet. I could tell my Grampy was feeling the same way. I shook hands with my last opponent and moved over to a place where I could watch Jack and his last opponent finish up. Jack's game went to a time scramble, which meant he had to move fast to finish before he ran out of time. He looked as if he was not having a good time. In the end it was a draw, meaning no one was the winner. They were tied. Jack just seemed happy to have it all over.

After the game, my mom told me that she and Mrs. James had gotten a lot of information about the next tournaments. I could tell that my mom was very proud of herself for getting all this stuff for me. Mrs. James said that a lot of the kids in the tournaments were on teams from different schools and some of the teams even had special banners. This was really big stuff. I kind of wished that our school could have a team. So far the only other kids that I knew of who played in our school had learned from our guidance counselor. Sometimes they go and see her and they play. Tommy told me that.

Stand Tall, Harry

After Jack and I poked around for a while, we all went up to this little restaurant in the hotel and had a very late lunch. The menu was kind of funny because it was all about kings and queens. Jack and I each had a Mighty King Burger, which came with great fries and then some not-so-great coleslaw. While the adults talked, Jack and I went back over our moves in our first-round games. Jack said he was kind of nervous having people watch and that he wasn't sure he liked playing in front of them all. I told him that at first I felt the same way, but as I got into the game I kind of forgot about all the people. I told him that my opponent had these kind of robot eyes and so I did the same thing she did. Jack said his opponent kept giving him these really serious looks and Jack kind of let his mind get the best of him. My dad always says that chess is a mind game. He says that you really have to check out of everything else to get into the game.

On the way home, my dad told me that there was a tournament the next Saturday at another place closer to Boston. I told him I would think about whether I wanted to play or not. I was feeling a little sad that Jack did not enjoy the tournament and might not want to continue. Part of what made it fun was having Jack doing it, too. I thought I wanted to play in more tournaments, and I was hoping that I could change Jack's mind.

My dad got right into my head and the next thing I knew he said, "You know, Harry, even if Jack might decide not to do any more tournaments, he could still come and watch you if he wanted. Then he could spend the weekend with us."

Can you believe that? How do parents do that, anyway? I decided to close my eyes and pretend I was asleep. Next thing I know, he'd probably be able to tell me what I was dreaming!

When we got home, I looked at the clock and started to think about hockey again and it made me sad. I was so hot for this season and I had practiced the whole month of August, nearly every day. This was to be a big year in hockey and now I was out. This was a big disappointment. I missed hangin' out at the rink with the older hockey players and having them give me high-fives. Even if I went to watch when I was feeling better, it wouldn't be the same. Hank and Herbie called to see if I wanted to hang out, but I decided to pass. I was feeling kind of down.

Sunday seemed like kind of a long day until Hank and Herbie stopped by. Hank came in and talked to me about how I was doing without hockey and Herbie headed to the kitchen to check out what my mom had baked. I ended up rapping with Hank about my chess tournament and how worried I was that Jack might quit going. Hank was so great. He kept talkin' about hockey and how he and Herbie don't play but still liked to see me play.

"Harry, it's all about being one of the brothers and Jack is one now, too," said Hank. "He can still go to the tournaments and not play in them. He's cool. He's cool. I know he'd want to do that."

As soon as Herbie heard "cool," he called from the kitchen that he was on his way. Hank and I started to cut up laughing. Herbie is so into himself, at least that's how he plays it. I've known these guys since we were in baby carriages. I'm so happy they didn't ditch me when I went off to my country school. Ya know, that happens to a lot of the kids who go out to other schools. When they're home on the weekends, they don't seem to be able to pick up with their old friends. I know kids who this had happened to, but Herbie and Hank are my brothers and we made a pact when we were little that nothing would ever break up the brothers, not even a new school.

It was a little weird when I first started going to my school in the burbs because they kept asking me why I left our school in Boston, kind of actin' like our old school wasn't good enough. But then it was okay. I explained to them that it wasn't that the school I went to was better; it was just a different experience for me. Sometimes it's good and sometimes it's not so good, same as any school.

After Herbie and Hank left, I took my shower and did my reading for school. Dad came in just as I was closing my book and asked me if I wanted to have a quick chess match. At first I wasn't sure because I was still kind of in a funk about Jack.

"Harry, how about just a quick one? If we don't finish, we can play the rest tomorrow."

My dad is great about getting me to do things that I might not think I want to do.

"Well, maybe I'll play for just a little while. I'm kind of tired."

"No problem, Harry. We can stop whenever you want as long as it's not because you're losing," and with that my dad gave out one of his belly laughs.

"Well, aren't we the comedian tonight, H. P. Junior," my mom called out from the kitchen.

Starting the chess game was a great idea and it made me think more about chess and how exciting the tournament had been and how proud I felt when I won. I ended up playing out the whole game with my dad and I even beat him. My dad is not easy to beat, so I was "king," at least for one night.

"Harry! Harry! Time to get up. This is the third time I've called you!"

I was in the middle of that same dream I had on the bus that day when Mr. Barrett woke me. Each time I wake up just when I am about to find out if I won the big tournament or not. If only everybody would just let me keep sleeping so I can finish my dream!

I began to open my eyes slowly and the first thing I saw were my mom's kneecaps staring me in the face. Then there seemed to be white everywhere.

"Mom has her uniform on all set to go to the hospital," I thought to myself, "and her last challenge before leaving is getting me out of bed."

As I dragged myself out of the bed, I could hear my dad cutting up in the kitchen with Grampy. My mom hates it if anybody is late, because then she feels like she already used up time that she never got to spend. I know that's kind of confusing, but I hope you get what I mean.

It was a rainy, dark day and just thinking about sitting on a bus for an hour-plus was making me wish I was back in the bed. As I headed for the bathroom, Mom reminded me that I had a doctor's appointment in the afternoon.

Chapter Twelve

"Oh no!" I thought to myself. "I'm going to be on auto pilot for the whole day and then some. What a long day it will be."

I hardly even remembered breakfast. I had to gobble my oatmeal down so fast that I felt like I had one of those fishing sinkers in my stomach. By the time I got on the bus, I was ready for bed again.

"Harry. Slow down. You look like you jogged the mile to get here today."

"Morning, Mr. Barrett. I overslept this morning so I've been rushing around since I got up."

"Well, Harry, seems you're not alone. Jeb's mother came to the bus stop in her bathrobe to tell me he's so late he couldn't make the bus. You both must have been havin' the same dream, except yours ended early enough for you to make it to the bus."

"Now how does Mr. Barrett know I was dreamin'?" I thought to myself.

I was beginning to feel like everyone always knows what I'm doing. I wish they had a crystal ball and could tell me how my dream ends. Then I'd definitely think that they were all right out of some science fiction story.

My bus ride seemed to go on forever. They were doing construction work and kept making us take new roads which Mr. Barrett had a hard time with because he doesn't know all these country ways. When we finally rounded the corner and I saw my school, I think Mr. Barrett was even more excited than the rest of us.

"Have a good day, Harry, and wish me luck on finding my way back to Boston."

Mr. Barrett was kind of laughing and kind of not laughing, all at the same time. I never ever saw Mr. Barrett in a funk. He's a lot like my Grampy. He told us once that he didn't have any children and so he drives the bus so he can say that now he has kids around. Mom can remember when he drove a city bus. Then he retired and started driving the students in our program out to their schools.

When I walked into my class, everyone was already on the rug and it was time to share about our weekend. Jack announced that I had won a chess tournament we had both played in. He was more excited than I had ever seen him during sharing. Mrs. Lamont asked me if I wanted to add anything. I don't really like doing a lot of talking so early in the morning, but today I kind of liked it and I just took off and went with it. Mrs. Lamont explained about how playing chess was like some of our "think cards" in math. You really have to use all your thinking skills and be able to predict where your move would get you. She said that just like there are a lot of different ways to solve our math problems, there are also a lot of different moves in chess that can help you win the game. Math was a subject I enjoyed so I was really getting into her talk.

As I was walking back to my desk, Jack whispered "Indoor recess, chess!" Then I remembered that I had forgotten to put my chess set in my bag. I knew that Mrs. Lamont had a chess game in the classroom, but I really liked playing on the magnetic board that Jack gave me.

"Jack," I whispered, "I think I left my magnetic board at home."

"No problem, Harry. We can use the one in the classroom."

Jack is a great problem solver. I might think there's a problem but he always seems to fix it before it becomes a problem. So then, there's really no problem. Get it?

Later on in the morning, when I went out to get my snack, I found my magnetic chess set in my backpack. My mom had attached a sticky note to it that said, "Have a good day, chess king!" I stood there looking at it with a big smile on my face. Mrs. Lamont was standing at the doorway and I could tell she had also read the note just by the look on her face. She didn't say a word, we just looked at each other, grinning, and I went in and had my snack.

When morning recess came, Jack asked Mrs. Lamont if we could go out in the back hall and play our chess game. I was happy playing right inside the room and I was wondering what was up with Jack. As we were setting up the board, Jack said, "You know, Harry, you and I are different. I get really nervous in front of people and you don't. I was awake the whole night before that chess tournament because I was so nervous about people watching me play. If you hadn't been playing, too, I know I never could have done it."

Chapter Twelve

I looked over at Jack and I thought he had tears in his eyes. I knew how hard it must have been for him to say this to me. Jack is a top student, a really outgoing kid, he never disses anybody, he takes on anything, and here he was telling me that he gets nervous playing in a chess tournament.

Instead of playing chess, we ended up talking about this for most of recess. Jack was worried that I might give up something that I was really good at just because he didn't want to do it. He even said he would try to go to some of my tournaments if I would just promise to keep playing in them. When we stopped talking, he had me so pumped up about chess that I couldn't wait for the next tournament.

When I got back to my seat and continued doing my morning work, I couldn't stop thinking about how hard it must be for Jack to get so worked up when people were watching him. Then I started to remember different things in class and how Mrs. Lamont never made Jack stand up in front of the room and speak. Then I thought about this morning and how excited she got when Jack started talking about the tournament. It all made sense to me. Mrs. Lamont was so good at covering that I never would have noticed anything if Jack and I didn't have our talk. The things we never know about each other! Here I thought I knew everything about my friend Jack.

Before long, it was time for me to pack up and get myself down to the cafeteria for the bus. While Jack was walking me down to the bus helping me with all my stuff, he started talking about the chess tournaments again. I could tell that he was really pumped.

Mr. Barrett was right on time and so our bus left pretty soon after the bell rang. I remembered my doctor's appointment on the way home. It was a pain to have such a long ride home and then get in another vehicle and have yet another ride and then a doctor's appointment on top of that. I tried to sleep a little on the bus, but I kept thinking about chess and all the different moves. My mind felt like a chessboard. Since Jeb had a Monday activity, I had a lot of time on the bus to think or to snooze.

Mom was waiting at the bus stop. Mr. Barrett offered to help me off, but I didn't have a lot to carry. I knew the other kids wanted to get home, anyway. We all want to get home as fast as we can because we spend so much time riding on the bus.

After I got into the car, my mom told me that Dr. Roberts might want me to have some X rays. When I asked what an X ray was, she told me that they are like films.

"Films," I thought to myself. "Why doesn't he just go rent some at the video store?"

I was pretty quiet for the rest of the ride and happy that my mom didn't ask me any more questions or talk to me much.

When we got to the hospital, we checked in first with Dr. Roberts's receptionist, who said he wanted to examine me before the X rays to be sure I was comfortable. The reception-ist told us that Dr. Roberts was on time and brought us into one of the examining rooms. I knew that was what they called those little rooms because it said so on the door. Dr. Roberts came right in and chatted with us as if we were old friends.

He examined me very carefully and told me that he wanted the X rays not just for the scoliosis, but to be sure my injuries had healed properly. He told me that clavicle fractures usually heal just fine and so he was not at all concerned. Then he began talking to me some more about scoliosis and told me that he had it himself when he was a little older than me. He said that it was probably idiopathic scoliosis, but it could be juvenile idiopathic scoliosis, which usually affects younger kids. He also explained that what they saw the night of my injury might not be scoliosis at all, but just my spine's reaction to the injury.

While he talked, my mom kept nodding her head, so I guessed Dr. Roberts was making sense to somebody in the room. I was a little confused, myself. I kept wondering whether to be worried. I was kind of half and half, half worried and half not worried.

"Before you go to X ray, Harry, I'd like to ask you to do a little bending for me. If you don't mind, I'm going to ask you to take off your shirt and bend forward for me in a dive posi-tion," said Dr. Roberts.

Chapter Twelve

As I bent over, I could feel Dr. Roberts's eyes studying my back. At one point he put his hand on my spine and I could feel him following it down to my waist. My mom was unusually quiet. Then Dr. Roberts said something to her about my waist and something about me not being that flexible. My mom just listened. I didn't like her being so quiet all of a sudden. Finally, he spoke to me.

"Harry, I know you're probably wondering what we're saying back here. I would like to get just a standing X ray of your back. You're going to be standing up in different positions. I will need to see you in about four weeks, Harry, just to give your injuries one last check. I'll study your pictures and compare them to the ones that were done the night of your accident and see if you definitely have scoliosis. There are a few things about your examination that suggest the possibility. I don't want you worrying about this, Harry. We can talk in more detail the next time I see you."

The X-ray room was down the hall pretty far from Dr. Roberts's area. While I changed into a johnny, which is one of those robe things that cover you up, my mom waited outside. Then I went into a room that felt kind of cold. The technician put this heavy weighted thing over me and then had me stand in different positions. Each time she took a picture, she went into this little box and switched the machine on and off. There was also a big table in the room. The technician said that some kids had to lie down on the table to be X-rayed. I was happy to be standing up.

After the technician finished, she asked me to wait outside so that she could be sure my X rays came out okay. After a few minutes she came back and said that I could get dressed and go. It was really pretty easy stuff.

On the way home, Mom talked to me about Consuela's scoliosis. I didn't remember much about it. Mom said that Grampy used to babysit me while she and my dad took Consuela to her appointments. I always thought Consuela looked pretty good, so I didn't know she had anything wrong with her. I was kind of excited that we might have the same thing because Consuela is my half-sister and this would make her even more than half, at least to me.

Chapter Thirteen

I listened carefully and I could tell that
Consuela was telling me everything.

As we pulled into the driveway, Grampy waved from the front steps. I could tell that he had been worrying about why we had been gone so long just for a doctor's visit.

"Where's everybody been? I thought you forgot what street you lived on," Grampy said half laughing and looking a little worried.

"Now, Dad. I told you that Harry might have a few X rays when I left to get him at the bus. I don't think you're hearing me anymore."

Before Grampy even got a chance to answer my mom, I interrupted.

"Mom, I'm going in to work on the computer," I called out.

I could tell Grampy wanted to talk to me, but all I wanted to do was get on the computer and let Consuela know that I might have scoliosis, too. Just as I was finishing up the E-mail to Consuela, my dad came in. I was pretty sure he thought I was E-mailing Jack since Jack and I just got the E-mail thing going between us.

"Harry, I hear you had a big day at the hospital. Seems that you and your sister might have similar backs."

Just as my dad finished his sentence, the phone rang. I raced to get it, hoping that it was Consuela. I had a feeling she'd call as soon as she got my E-mail. Normally she calls once a week, on the weekend, but I thought she'd be able to tell that I needed to talk to her.

"Hello."

"Harry, it's Consuela. I just got your E-mail about your back and the X rays. I can tell you're a little worried about maybe having scoliosis and especially wondering if you might need a brace at some point."

I took the phone into my bedroom as I talked and shut the door behind me, hoping that my dad wouldn't follow. I knew Consuela would answer my questions. Besides the girl in school with the back brace, there had been a girl in a brace at the chess tournament on Saturday. The brace came up under her chin and she looked kind of uncomfortable. They made the chessboard higher so she could see it more easily. My mind was just racing with questions.

"Harry, I have had scoliosis for a long, long time. I was eight when they diagnosed mine and they called it juvenile idiopathic scoliosis. Our pediatrician saw it and told Mom and Dad that I needed to go see another doctor. I saw the doctor in the same place your doctor is. I had X rays, the whole bit, Harry. Then for years I went every six months for X rays and once they took some MRIs, another kind of picture. They'd always measure my arms, my feet, my legs; it seemed like they measured everything. A few times the curve got worse, but not enough to need a brace. Just when it started getting close to that I stopped growing, and then it didn't move much. Now I just have it checked once every few years. I'm not even sure I need to do that, but I promised Mom and Dad I would keep going."

I listened carefully and I could tell that Consuela was telling me everything. One thing about Consuela, she always tells the truth. We rapped about some other stuff, too. Mom was calling out for dinner and I could hear my dad hushing her.

"Harry, lots of kids have scoliosis," Consuela continued. "First, wait and see. If you do have it, it's going to be okay. I have known kids who have even worn braces and they do fine. They don't like having to wear the brace, but their clothes hide it."

"That's not true, Consuela," I replied. "I saw a girl wearing a brace at my chess tournament and you could see part of it under her chin."

"Harry, did she win?"

"Well, yeah, she did," I answered, ready to diss my sister for changing the subject.

"Harry, that's called a Milwaukee brace and I knew someone who had one of those, too. She was captain of the swim team. When she needed to swim or practice, she just took the brace off. Harry, she did just fine."

"Okay, Consuela. I just can't stop thinking about it. I'm still pretty upset about my hockey accident and now this on top of it. It feels like all the bad stuff is happening to me."

"Harry, I understand how you feel, but wait until you see your doctor again. Don't start worrying until you have something for sure to worry about. Call me back and then we'll worry together, okay?"

"Boy, if she doesn't sound like Mom," I thought to myself.

"Harry, I hear you're a chess king, now. I want to hear about it," continued Consuela.

I began telling Consuela about my tournament and just when I was getting into the good part, Mom knocked on the door and told me we had to eat. Dad came in behind her and I kind of knew they might have heard what I was talking to Consuela about. They had that "We're cool, we're not gonna ask any questions" look on their faces. I handed the phone to Dad so he could say a quick hello to Consuela and went in to wash my hands for dinner.

Dinner was far-out. Grampy, who reads the obituary part of the newspaper first each day (that's the part that tells who died), just took off on this lady who had just died named Frances R. Horwich. I guess she had this program for kids that was on TV long before *Mr. Rogers* and *Sesame Street.* Get this. Her show was called *Ding Dong School.* Grampy said his aunt's kids used to watch it every morning back in the 1950s. Having a TV at all back in those days was something according to Grampy. He said that this Miss Frances even had pets on the show, but I don't think they were real. Grampy remembered their names, Jocko the monkey and Lucky the rabbit. Even my mom was getting into this, but she couldn't remember the show. By the time dinner ended, I thought they had all gone "Ding Dong"! Ya think?

After dinner, it was time for homework. I had to write a paragraph for Mrs. Lamont about, get this, "A Memorable Family Time." I just busted up and I decided to write about Grampy and this "Ding Dong" lady because I knew this was a dinner I would never forget. Here I was going from worrying about scoliosis to hearing about the death of a "Ding Dong" lady who I never even heard of before.

"Wait till Mrs. Lamont reads this!" I thought to myself.

My homework was going fast, even my new math problems on fractions. Just when I started to pack up my backpack for school, which I had to do every night before I went to bed, my dad wandered in.

"Harry, we haven't even had a minute to talk about your appointment today with Dr. Roberts. If I could have arranged my schedule to go with you, son, I would have."

"No problem, Dad. I was kind of surprised myself about getting the X rays today, but Consuela says it worked out for the better because I didn't have time to get all worried about it all. Maybe she's right. And besides, X rays are easy."

"Well, Harry, from what your mom reported to me, it sounds like you and your sister have more and more in common. The only difference seems to be that your body is a lot more muscular than hers. I'm sure she told you, Harry, that for years we went to have her back checked and only twice did her curve show what they called 'progression,' meaning that it increased. After that, it seemed to stay just the way it is now. Your mom still asks Consuela to have it checked every few years, but she never needed anything but X rays and monitoring by the doctor."

Chapter Thirteen

I was starting to feel sort of okay about the scoliosis because they weren't even sure I had it. Having my dad tell me the same stuff about scoliosis that Consuela told me, and having Consuela say the same stuff that Dr. Roberts said, made me feel that everybody was telling me the truth. I guess that's a kid thing, needing to keep checking around. Whatever. All I knew was that I felt better since I had talked to Consuela.

After our talk my dad said he had something to show me. He went out and got his work briefcase and pulled out a bunch of papers on chess tournaments in Massachusetts. There were two coming up this weekend. One had a Game in sixty minutes Time Limit and the other had one of a Game in ninety minutes. One was way early in the morning on Saturday and the first round for the other was ten o'clock.

"Harry, it's up to you, son. If you don't want to do this anymore I certainly don't want to push you. I just got the information for you, that's all."

I quickly replayed in my mind my conversation with Jack. He had really pumped me up for another chess tournament and it was a game I really loved.

"I think I do want to do it, Dad. I just don't want to have to go too early in the morning."

I could tell my dad was pumped, too. When I looked down I could see he had even filled out part of each application. I decided to pretend I didn't see it, especially when he said, "While you get ready for bed, I'll fill out the application, Harry."

Parents! As Herbie would say, "Sometimes their clues are so out there that they are jumpin' in your face!"

My week at school seemed to fly by. I was feeling more comfortable and Jack and I played chess at both morning and lunch recess, with Tommy glued to our board not saying anything, but doing a lot of nodding. I felt that Jack was becoming my chess coach. He told me he had been going on-line and learning new moves. Some of them I already knew, but I would never say that to Jack.

When Saturday came, Jack's mom and dad dropped him off on their way to do an errand in the city. At first, I didn't know he had arrived because I was in the shower. When I got out, dressed, and pulled up the shade, I could see Jack sitting on the front stoop. Grampy was probably telling Jack how much time we spend on that stoop and how important it is to "stand tall" and be proud of who you are. I looked at Jack's face, sitting there listening to my Grampy, and I could see myself doing the same thing. My Grampy is like a magnet. Everyone is attracted to him and everyone loves him, especially me.

Just like last week, our whole family and now Jack, too, piled into the car for the tournament. It was a little squeezed in the backseat, but my dad said it would be a short ride. Well, it was a really short ride and we got there so fast I felt like I almost wasn't ready.

While Grampy and Mom checked out the place, Dad and Jack came with me while I checked in. I noticed some of the same faces that had been at the last tournament. We had a very short wait and then the time came for me to go in. I sat down at my board number, but my opponent wasn't there yet. Then a man came over and gave me a different chair and changed the chessboard and the table. Pretty soon that same girl with the Milwaukee brace from the last tournament came over and sat down. I could see why they changed everything around. She looked over at me with a kind of "I'm sorry" look on her face and it made me feel bad. I turned my head to look at Jack and instead caught my Grampy's eye. I could tell he was feeling bad for her and I also knew he wanted me to say something to make her feel better. I could just see it in Grampy's eyes.

I started to tell her my name, and as I was reaching over to shake her hand, I got a sharp pain and knocked over two chess pieces. We both started giggling and then, I don't know where it came from, but I said to her, "Between my sore self and your brace, this is going to be quite a game."

"Egad," I thought to myself. "If this isn't a 'take-backer' I don't know what is!"

Oh how I wished I had kept my big mouth shut. I looked over at her and she had this big grin on her face. I had "broken the ice," just what was needed.

Her name was Dawn and I soon found out that she was a great chess player. I didn't think we would ever finish our game. Finally, it was a draw, meaning neither of us won, but we kind of both did. My dad said after the game that we were "evenly matched," which meant that we both did a good job.

As Dawn was carefully getting off her chair, she looked at me and said, "Thank you, Harry. You made this fun for me today. Usually I feel kind of weird in front of everyone because of my brace. Today, I didn't feel weird."

And then something came out of my mouth almost out of nowhere.

"Well, you know, Dawn. I might have scoliosis, too."

Dawn looked shocked and quickly answered, "Really?"

"Yeah, I might, and my sister has it, too."

"Well, Harry, mine is pretty serious, so I'm going to be having an operation soon. I'm wishing the operation can wait until after this special chess tournament I hope to be invited to play in. My dad kind of got me into this when my brace went on because I used to do gymnastics and now with the brace, it's kind of hard."

"Ya want to hear something funny, Dawn? My dad kind of got me into this because I had a hockey injury and couldn't play hockey this season."

Dawn smiled and as she started to walk away she said, "Well, then, I guess we may be playing together again, Harry Jones. See you at the next competition."

On the way home, I told Jack and everyone about my talk with Dawn. I was kind of happy about not being the only one at a tournament with something wrong, if you know what I mean. Jack said that Dawn and I might be opponents at other meets because we play about the same. In the back of my mind I kept thinking of what she said about wanting to win this big tournament, although I never asked her the name of it.

Jack loved being in Boston, and he and I and Herbie and Hank had so much fun together. After my chess tournament, we finally got over to Herbie's to watch a movie, one that his brother got. Jack's eyes were as big as dinner plates as he watched the four generations of people who are always around Herbie's house and all the talkin', talkin', talkin' that goes on.

When it was time to leave, I could tell Jack would have been just as happy staying at Herbie's for the night. Finally, Herbie's dad walked us home. Even though we weren't that far from our house, it was late and Grampy and my mom's rule is that we never walk home alone.

The next morning Jack ended up coming to church with us. Grampy offered to stay home and play a game of chess with him.

"Jack, you don't know what you're getting yourself into, son," said Grampy. "You're going to be singing to sweet Jesus for three hours and you're going to hear enough hallelujahs to last your whole life."

Just as Grampy finished, Mom gave him one of her looks and that was the end of church talk. Next thing I knew, my Grampy was sending us out the door telling Jack that church was great and it was really a good time. I saw the funny look my mom gave my dad as we all paraded out the door.

Chapter Fourteen

I finally had a real routine to my life: a friend at school, Jeb to talk to on the bus, and my chess tournaments. Even though I missed hockey and I still went to watch some of the games and practices, chess had really taken its place. At least for this year.

In school, whenever Jack was out or busy, I kept teaching Tommy how to play chess. Tommy had a good head and he was learning a lot just by watching Jack and me. He seemed a lot calmer and Jack and I continued trying to help him so he didn't call out so much. I had to give my Grampy the points for this. At least once a week since the snack incident, Grampy and I have a "Tommy talk" on the front stoop. My Grampy always tells me a story about someone he knew when he was in school who was like Tommy. Grampy always ends the "Tommy talk" by telling me to help Tommy to "stand tall."

"Harry, you can help him with this, I just know you can, son," said Grampy.

No one will ever stand as tall as my Grampy. His heart is as big as he is tall.

My injury was coming along and I felt pretty normal except when I twisted my body quickly. Then I knew something was still not exactly right. Soon I had to go to see Dr. Roberts. Both my mom and dad were going to the appointment with me because Dr. Roberts would be talking about the results of the X rays. My parents would meet my bus and then we would go into the hospital from there. Another one of those long days!

When I got to school, I found out Mrs. Lamont was changing our seats. She does this once a month and we all get to choose three names of people we want to sit next to. I put down Tommy, Susan, and Joshua. I didn't put down Jack because I had been near him for the last month and once before, too. I knew I wouldn't have him in my group again for a while. My new group ended up being Susan, Molly, Tommy, and me. The girls didn't look too happy about Tommy, especially Susan. Tommy didn't look too happy either because of the Susan snack incident. It sure was going to be an interesting month, though a short one because of the holidays. It might turn out to be one of the longest months if the grouping didn't go well.

In science we were planting seeds for something called "fast plants." Some of us had special things called variables that we would be doing with our plants. Our group was putting extra food in our plants to see if it helped them to grow faster. Some of the other variables were more light and then this cellophane cover that was kind of purple. Some groups had no variables at all. We each got a notebook in which to report on what we observed with our plants and write in it three times a week. Since my Grampy has always had a big garden in the back of our brownstone, I was really excited about all this. I knew quite a bit about plants already, which kind of surprised Susan. She must have thought that Boston is all sidewalks and cement! I know lots of beautiful gardens in the back of houses in my neighborhood. Country people think the city is so different from the country, but in a lot of ways, the city and the country can be kind of the same. The big difference is that in the country you have more open land, more green, fewer buildings, and no street lights, so when it is dark, it is really dark.

After our seeds were planted, we had snack and then headed out to recess. I grabbed my chess set and Jack and I headed for the wall. Tommy, who usually watched us, tried to get into a kickball game. Amazing! Susan picked him for her team! I think it was because he helped her plant her seeds in class. Wait until my Grampy heard this!

The rest of the day went pretty fast: rehearsal for the music program, read another chapter in *Number the Stars*, math, and writing. I was happy to be on the bus heading home so I could have a little rest before my doctor's appointment. Jeb was at another afternoon activity so the bus ride was pretty quiet. In the middle school, where Jeb is, there are activities almost every afternoon. It sounded awesome!

Chapter Fourteen

Mom and Dad were waiting for me at the bus. Dad got out of the car and said a quick hello to Mr. Barrett and then off we went. I told them all about my fast plants and my new group.

"Wow, Harry. Sounds like a great day just moving your seat and planting seeds. Sure took a long time to do it all, didn't it?"

That was my dad's way of dissing me because he wanted more detail about my day. Parents!

We were at the hospital in no time. Dr. Roberts was a little backed up so the receptionist said we might have about a fifteen-minute wait. I just sat there watching patients come in with broken legs, broken arms, back braces, and some other unusual-looking contraptions that I guessed were supposed to be helping them. Looked kind of scary to me!

"What a strange place this is," I thought to myself. "I sure hope I don't join this group and get something of my own to wear."

Pretty soon the receptionist came over and brought us to an examining room. I changed into a johnny and in a few minutes Dr. Roberts came in. He came over and shook my hand and then did the same with my dad, saying hello to my mom almost at the same time. He asked me to lie down on the examining table and started to check me out. He said that he thought I was doing pretty well and that the X ray also indicated that things were healing nicely. Then he turned on the light box in the examining room and showed us the pictures of my back.

Dr. Roberts explained that I had a structural scoliosis of about 20° — with some apex vertebral rotation in the direction of the scoliosis. Rotation, he explained, is when the vertebral column turns around its axis, whatever that is. Dr. Roberts went on to say that there was no evidence of any other malformations and that he had no way of knowing whether the curve would progress. He suggested that I return in about six months and then he would decide whether I needed to see him less often. Then he turned to me and started to talk as if he and I were alone. He really made me feel important.

"Harry, I want to be sure you understand what scoliosis is," he began.

"Scoliosis is curvature of the spine. The spine is this bony structure you feel down the middle of your back. No one actually knows where scoliosis comes from, but the research is now telling us that in some cases, scoliosis can be in your family. I know your sister has it and I think your mom said that your sister was actually seen in this clinic. From what your mom says, your sister's curve progressed, but not enough to need bracing. I have no crystal ball to tell you exactly what your spine will do, Harry. Your body is very muscular and you're already a tall boy, which tells me that you have already had an early growth spurt. If this continues, your curve may also grow or as we say, 'progress.' No one can say, Harry. At this point, no one will even know you have scoliosis because your curve is very slight. I'll see you in about six months for the scoliosis and in about four weeks to give your clavicle fracture one last check. Any questions?"

"Does this mean I can play hockey again?" I asked.

"Actually, no it doesn't, Harry. You aren't going to be ready for any contact sport for a while. I have a feeling you won't be back in the game this season, but I do think you can resume some skating, maybe in about six weeks."

Before I could say anything else, my dad told Dr. Roberts that I had become a "chess king." I wanted to go hide someplace. My dad went on to tell him I had already played in two tournaments.

"Turn him off," I thought to myself.

My dad was really on a roll. Mom could see I was not any too happy about this chess talk and so she finally said, "Thank you so much, Dr. Roberts. We know you have other patients to see so we'll get going."

The look on my dad's face was so funny. He was not ready to stop, that's for sure. My mom just took his arm and led him out of the room.

Dr. Roberts looked over at me and said, "Chess, wow, Harry. Now that is a very difficult game and one that I know a little about. I used to play it with my dad many, many years ago. Good luck with your next tournament. I'll see you in four weeks."

On the way home, I knew my parents wanted to have some talk about scoliosis, but I just closed my eyes and pretended I had checked out. I'd had enough hospital talk for one day.

Chapter Fourteen

When I got home, Grampy was sitting on the front step waiting to see how things went. I really didn't feel like talking to him about the visit and just when I was trying to figure out how to bypass him, the phone started ringing. Saved by the phone! I rushed up the steps to get it.

It was Jack pretending he was someone doing a survey on chess players from the Boston area. At first he had me going. Then, when he asked if I thought city boys were better players than country boys, I knew it had to be a crank call or someone playing a joke on me. So I played along and told him that "burb boys" play chess about as well as they play street hockey! Jack got really defensive and told me there were streets in the country, too, and then I knew it had to be him.

It felt good to laugh a little and to get back into stuff that didn't have anything to do with doctors. I knew Jack was calling to see how I made out, but I also knew he wouldn't pump me and he would definitely take the short answer.

"So, how did you make out at the doctor's, Harry? Do you definitely have scoliosis?" he asked.

"Yeah, Jack, I do. But I was pretty sure I did even before I went because my sister has it, too. My parents are so into this with me, but I don't want to think about it. It's kind of like giving up hockey for this year. I just want to move on for now."

"Harry, I'm the same. My parents used to ask me all these questions about not liking to talk in front of the class and stuff. Finally, they stopped, and I like it a lot better, now."

Jack and I only talked for a few more minutes because it was a long distance call and kind of expensive. I told him I would E-mail him after dinner if I had some time.

Just as I was hanging up with Jack, the doorbell rang. It was Herbie and Hank.

"What are they doing here at dinnertime on a school night?" I thought to myself.

"So, Harry, here's the deal. If you do have that scoliosis thing you were talking about, I found two kids at school who have it, too, and they'll come talk to you whenever you want."

This came out of Herbie like one long sentence and he never stopped once to take a breath.

"He's probably been rehearsing it all day," I thought to myself.

Hank and I stood there smiling at each other.

"Herbie, that is really nice of you. Is that why you guys are over here on a school night?"

"Well, Harry, we've been feeling like everything is happening to you," Hank answered, "and so we decided we'd better stop by and see how you made out today."

"Thanks guys, thanks so much. It really means a lot to me."

Grampy went over and put his arm around each of them and said, "Well, that's what the brothers are all about, isn't it boys?"

After dinner, Dad and I signed me up on the Internet for another chess tournament. This one was farther away and was supposed to be a really good one. I read about it in the chess magazine and it seemed like lots of kids went to raise their ratings. Chess is sweet!

School started to by go faster and faster. I played in chess tournaments most weekends and Jack came to quite a few of them. At one I earned not only a pretty good rating, but a trophy, too. Only Dad came to that one, so for the rest of the next week I listened to Mom and Grampy beating up on themselves for not coming. My house always has humor in it, for sure.

By the time Thanksgiving came, Tommy knew not only how to play chess, but how to play it well. He and Jack switched off and he started playing more games with me with Jack serving as his coach. In fact, Jack and I decided Tommy could come to my next tournament with Jack if he wanted to and Mom said both he and Jack could spend the night. I couldn't wait to see Herbie with Tommy. That would be something! They'd either be dissing each other or dissing everybody around them!

What always makes Thanksgiving for me is all the people who come and eat with us. My Grammy was like the big lady at church when she was alive. She helped a lot of people. My mom still has the people over for Thanksgiving. Sometimes she cooks three turkeys and then we borrow more tables and chairs from church. Grampy makes the vegetables all week long and all he and Mom talk about is food, food, food! Best of all is that my sister, Consuela, would be home and this year she would be bringing two friends who come from other countries. They never had a Thanksgiving dinner before.

It was a half day of school before Thanksgiving Day. The Boston bus was almost empty. Some of the kids were away and some just didn't want to sit on a bus for almost two and a half hours for just three hours of school. In my house, you go to school every day it's happenin' and that's it!

My classroom was also pretty empty. Jack was off to see his aunt and uncle and except for Tommy, no one was left in our group. Mrs. Lamont organized a game of social studies Jeopardy with teams. We were reviewing all our Canada stuff getting ready for the final test. Tommy was really on a roll and knew a lot of the answers. He always loves a good game.

The bus ride home was longer than I wished. There was already a lot of traffic and poor Mr. Barrett was not happy with all the out-of-state drivers. I kept thinking about how exciting it was going to be to have Consuela home and to meet her friends. She took a morning plane so she might be home even before me.

As Mr. Barrett pulled around the corner to the bus stop, Consuela was standing there with her friends with a big grin on her face. Mr. Barrett, who used to drive her, got all excited and he even got off the bus to give her a hug. Mom had given Consuela a zucchini bread for Mr. Barrett and when Consuela handed it to him, he got even more excited.

Consuela's new friends were so cool. One was from England and talked with this funny accent, almost cutting off her words, and the other friend was from France. Her English was kind of hard to understand, but Consuela could speak to her in French so that helped. On our way back to the house, I told them all about my chess tournaments and that I had won five of my first six games. Consuela was really excited for me. In fact, she told me that for years Dad wanted her to play, but it used to take too long. Finally, he gave up.

Thanksgiving ended up being the most amazing time ever. When Grampy said grace, we all joined hands and there were so many people in the room that it looked like this long snake. Grampy looked out at everybody as he was finishing all his "Thank you, Lords" and said, "Hopefully, Lord, each one of us will continue to stand tall and be proud of who we are."

I looked over at Consuela's friends and their eyes were all teary. My Grampy is about as special as they come and definitely the tallest man in the whole world.

The weekend after Thanksgiving, Tommy and Jack both planned to come for an overnight. I had never seen Tommy so out of his skin with excitement in all the time I had known him. Jack's dad drove them to my chess tournament and met us in the lobby. Then, when we walked into the tournament room, Tommy's eyes looked bigger than his head. He and Jack sat with my dad and Grampy and watched me for what turned out to be a very long game. I finally won, but my opponent came very close to beating me.

As we were leaving the tournament, Dawn met us at the door. She had her brace on and when Tommy saw it I was sure he would say something, but amazingly he didn't. Jack and I both looked at each other definitely thinking the same thing, "Tommy has come a long way."

Dawn told us about a chess club they were starting at her school and how her teacher was really helping to get it going. The PTO, a parents group, would be putting up the money. Dawn said they were paying this chess teacher to come one afternoon a week and teach everyone how to play.

On the way home in the car, Tommy started talking about chess clubs. I felt like he was reading my mind because I was thinking about them myself.

"Harry, you should ask Mrs. Lamont to help you to get a chess club started at our school. I bet lots of kids would like to learn how to play. You could help her, Harry, and I could tell her that Jack and I want one, too," said Tommy.

"You want one, don't you Jack?" Tommy asked waiting for Jack to agree with him. Tommy always needed to know that Jack was okay with something, too, maybe because Jack and I are such good friends.

Chapter Fourteen

"I think it's a great idea, Tommy," answered Jack and then my dad and my Grampy started talking about it, too. Our whole car ride back to Boston was about this chess club. By the time we got to my house, we even had the club named — the Mercier Movers — since our school is the Mercier School.

About ten minutes after we got home, Herbie and Hank arrived to check Tommy out. When Herbie asked Tommy how he liked going to a chess tournament, Tommy started telling him how this girl with a metal bar under her chin gave us a great idea to start a chess club. All Herbie heard was the metal bar part. Then he and Tommy spent the next ten minutes talking about Dawn's brace and how she could even play chess with the contraption. Finally, my mom interrupted and explained to both of them all about a Milwaukee brace and why Dawn was wearing it. This was one of the few times I was glad my mom brought her nursing skills to my rescue.

My mom had made homemade pizza and asked Herbie and Hank if they wanted to eat with us. Herbie wanted to know what was for dessert before he decided. When Mom said "chocolate fudge cake with maple walnut icing," Herbie was already at the table. We all started laughing.

Dinner rocked. I had all my friends in Boston eating my favorite dinner, and then my burb friends spending the night. I never thought this would happen. Never. Friends are so cool! Just as I was thinking this, Grampy walked by and whispered in my ear, "I bet you think life is pretty darn good right now, Harry Jones." Boy, can he get in my head!

Chapter Fifteen

*The PTO agreed to get a big plastic banner made
and to call the group the "Mercier Movers."*

By the time I went on Christmas vacation, I had gained
almost as many rating points as I needed to qualify for
something really big. It snowed a lot, so Jack didn't get into
Boston as much as we had planned over the Christmas break,
but he did get over once. I was finally back on skates again.
But even though I was allowed to skate, I didn't seem to have
the time. I spent most of it on the Internet checking out chess
games and playing with my dad and my Grampy. I even got
Hank and Herbie to start playing.

One really snowy day they came over and Grampy and I set
up the chessboard and the computer. They were hooked.
Grampy worked with Herbie on the magnetic board and I
worked with Hank using this web site that's all about learning
how to play chess. We had such an awesome day and by the

time my dad came home, Hank and Herbie pretty much knew how to play. When I E-mailed Jack and told him, he got excited, too.

In January, the PTO mother in charge of our monthly school newsletter asked if she could interview me. She said she kept hearing about me being a "chess king" and she thought it would be fun to do an article. So one day, during recess, she came and asked me all these questions. Mrs. Lamont sat in on the interview, too, which I was really happy about. I mean I didn't know this mom and all of a sudden I had to talk to her about chess.

Just when she was finishing up her interview, she looked me straight in the eye and said, "Harry, if you could do or change anything in the Mercier School, what would it be?"

My first thought was to have them move the school closer to Boston, but I was afraid she'd think I was giving her some smart-aleck answer. Finally, it just came out of nowhere.

"Well, if I could do anything I guess I'd start a chess club here at school. Most of the kids who play in the tournaments have chess clubs at their schools and some of them even hang banners with the name of their school chess club on them. I'd call our group the 'Mercier Movers.'"

She started to laugh when I told her what I had come up with. I told her it was the name that we thought of when Tommy and Jack came to one of my tournaments. Mrs. Lamont explained that Tommy and Jack were my classmates. When the interview was over, I felt really, really special.

During gym that afternoon, Mrs. Lamont asked me if I could join her and Mrs. Starck, our principal, while they talked about something special. At first, I felt very nervous, but Mrs. Lamont looked kind of excited, so it seemed okay to go. I knew I hadn't done anything wrong. On the way to the office, Mrs. Lamont started telling me that she wanted me to share my chess club idea with Mrs. Starck. The mom who had interviewed me thought that the PTO might be willing to help it get started.

I was a little nervous, but I kept telling myself what they told me in kindergarten when I first came to school, "Principal/pal,

Principal/pal." Mrs. Harrington, our Boston program coordinator, always said the principal was our pal and not the enemy.

When I went into Mrs. Starck's office, I noticed that on her
office bulletin board was a photo and article from our program
newsletter about me being the "chess king." I remembered
when the article came out back in early December. Mrs.
Lamont shared it with our class and I remembered Mrs. Starck
coming in and congratulating me, but I sure didn't think I'd be
hanging on her wall.

We had a really exciting meeting and I told them both about
how Jack and Tommy and I got this idea after one of my tournaments. When the meeting ended, they told me I could be
the "student liaison" for the club and that Tommy and Jack
could be my assistants.

"Harry, your job is going to be to talk this up and get kids to
join," Mrs. Lamont said as she and I got up to walk out. Then
she asked me if I knew of any chess teachers who might be
willing to come in and teach once a week after school. I knew
just the man. I thought he already taught in some schools. I
met him at a tournament and he gave my dad his card and
said that he taught lots of kids. I told Mrs. Lamont I would
bring her the card with his name and phone number on it.

"If he can't help us, Mrs. Lamont, he may be able to give us
another idea," I said.

"Sounds like a good plan to me, Harry," and when I turned
to see who said that, I saw Mrs. Starck standing behind us. I
guess she was behind us all the time and I didn't even know it.

"You know, Harry, as the school principal, I watch each child
very carefully and I know just about everything that is going
on with them. I happen to know that you took a pretty serious
injury and turned it around. I also know that you have become
a very good friend to Tommy, which did not start out well,
either. Mrs. Lamont told me about the snack incident. You
make us all proud, Harry, very proud."

I just stood there for a minute and finally I looked up at her
and said, "Thank you, Mrs. Starck." And when she walked
away I had this feeling inside me that was just amazing.
"School is really cool," I thought to myself. "It rocks so
much!"

I tried to tell Jack and Tommy a little about what happened with Mrs. Lamont and Mrs. Starck and the new chess club. I didn't have much time because we all had to pack up to leave. I thought Jeb was going to be on the bus and I couldn't wait to share it all with him, too. A chess club at my school. Hot!

I just about talked Jeb's ear off on the way home, but I knew he didn't mind. When they started a drama club at his school, he got just as excited as I was about the chess. He talked about it for days and I even helped him practice his lines for the first play he was in.

I kept on talking to Jeb as I was getting off the bus and I almost forgot my backpack. Jeb came running down the aisle chasing me with it while Mr. Barrett just sat there shaking his head.

When I got home, Grampy was watching the early afternoon news on TV. There was still a lot of snow around our house and it sure was cold out. The temperature had not been above freezing in over a week.

"Grampy, Grampy. Guess what? Mrs. Lamont and Mrs. Starck, the principal, and this PTO lady are going to let us start a chess club at school and I'm going to be the 'lason,' which is a really important job."

"Slow down, Harry. You told me about three different things in one sentence. And I have no idea what a 'lason' is. Are you sure that's something important?"

I sat down and started all over, telling my Grampy about the newsletter interview, which I had completely forgotten to tell Jeb. Then I told him about going into the principal's office with my teacher and looking up and seeing myself on her bulletin board. I still couldn't believe I was up there. Then I explained about how they were going to start the chess club and how I would help them and be the "lason" and Jack and Tommy, my helpers.

"Harry, it sounds like you're becoming a pretty important person in all this chess stuff, but the only thing that I am not at all sure about is this 'lason' thing. We'd better ask your dad about it."

Chapter Fifteen

When my dad came home, I met him at the front door and told him about my day. He was very excited for me, but he really started busting up when I told him about my job as the "lason" and how Grampy was a little worried that it might not be a good thing after all.

"Harry, the word is 'liaison' and it means that you are probably going to be the student representative for the club. This is all very exciting, son."

Mom came in late from the hospital and my dad let me stay up and tell her everything. She was really excited and told me that she'd let Mrs. Harrington know about the club.

"Harry, didn't I tell you that things would work out when you got hurt? This is even better than 'working out.' This rocks, Harry, it really rocks."

"Go Mom," I yelled out, and we all started laughing.

Between starting the chess club and playing in tournaments, my life was as busy as it had ever been. My routine seemed to be on fast-forward and Jack and Tommy ended up playing chess at recess while I got the chess club stuff going. Sometimes they helped me, like with signs and posters and stuff. The PTO agreed to get a big plastic banner and to call the group the "Mercier Movers." A few kids thought it sounded like a moving company, but I still liked it. I guess the reason I liked it the most was because the whole thing was started in the backseat of our car.

Mrs. Lamont contacted the chess instructor and he agreed to come one afternoon a week. He told her what we would need and about how much it would cost. The boards would be heavy vinyl and the pieces were made of plastic. The instructor said that our school could order the supplies from him and he would give us his discount. The PTO agreed to pay all the club expenses. Mrs. Starck said that we would announce the opening of the club at one of our Friday assemblies as soon as the banner was ready. I just couldn't believe all this was happening.

All through February we worked on getting the "Mercier Movers" off the ground and getting all the kids psyched about joining. Kids in the third and fourth grades could join. I wasn't so sure I could go because our school had no late bus back to the city. When I told Mrs. Lamont about it, she called Mrs. Harrington, who got right on it. The late bus would stop at Mercier on the way back from getting the middle school kids who had afternoon activities. That meant Jeb and I might be on the late bus together. Something else to be excited about!

In early March the banner was ready and the day finally came for the assembly when Mrs. Starck would announce the club. Mrs. Lamont told Jack, Tommy, and me to be prepared to go up on the stage with Mrs. Starck. Jack got so nervous he almost backed out, but then Mrs. Lamont talked to him and we decided to just stand in front of everyone and not up on the stage. Mrs. Lamont always knows how to fix things. Everything!

Most of the time when Mom tells me to wear nice clothes, I don't want to do it, but today was special and I would have picked them out on my own. For our assembly I wanted to look like one of those experienced chess players, if you know what I mean. This was a big day for me.

Mr. Barrett got us to school right on time. I could tell he knew something was up because I was carrying my good shoes and he could see I had my good pants on, too. As I was walking into the cafeteria, Tommy started waving like a wild man. He wanted me to meet his mom and dad. It was the first time either of them had been to school the whole year except maybe for conferences. I started right over to meet them and Jack joined me halfway as he was bringing some things into the auditorium for our assembly. He had a few chessboards and some chess pieces in his hands.

Meeting Tommy's parents was cool. They were really nice and I could tell they felt very proud of him. I kind of wished I had asked my own parents to come. I'd been so busy with the chess club that I never even thought about it. I was feeling a little sad. I was pretty sure Jack's parents weren't coming either because he was so nervous about this whole thing. But maybe they would be coming and he had just forgotten to tell me.

Chapter Fifteen

I told Tommy and Jack that I had to hurry and drop my stuff off because it was getting late and the assembly would start at nine o'clock sharp. Tommy followed me down to class and I couldn't remember a time that he looked so excited and so proud. When we got to class, everyone was getting ready for morning exercises. We quickly got into our places. When I looked over at Mrs. Lamont, I noticed that she had a special dress on and looked especially nice. Even her hair looked done up kind of different.

Shortly after our morning exercises, they called all the third-grade classes on the intercom to go to the auditorium. Even though the chess club was only for third and fourth graders, our assembly always includes the whole school. We usually talk about special things there. Mrs. Starck always says it is our chance to be together as a school family all in the same room at the same time.

Once all the grades were seated, Mrs. Starck greeted us and shared what we would be doing, which she called "celebrating" together. She really gets into these assemblies, big time! When it came time to announce the chess club, Mrs. Starck had two fourth graders come up first and hold the banner open. It looked just like a chessboard and in the middle were the king and queen chess pieces and around the top and the bottom was written "Mercier Movers."

Jack, Tommy, and I were standing to the side while Mrs. Starck said all these embarrassing things about us. All three of us got to say a few words. Mrs. Starck asked me to tell everyone how I got into chess. When I started to tell them, I picked my head up and looked out into the audience and way in the back I could see my Grampy, my parents, and Mrs. Harrington. My eyes met my Grampy's as I talked and for just a minute I felt like my Great-Grampy was in the room with me, too. When I finished talking, everyone started to clap. I could feel my face getting so red. I get red when there's such a big deal. Tommy got to speak next and he told everyone how he finally had friends and how he wanted to be like us in every way, including knowing how to play chess. I looked out at his parents and they looked so proud of him. Tommy was finally "standing tall" and feeling "very proud of who he is."

When it came time for Jack to speak, at first he didn't take the microphone. Then Mrs. Lamont came over and put her arm on his shoulder and he began. He talked about that first chess tournament we went to and how sometimes he got nervous and how he didn't want to try things, but that we all really should give things a chance. Then he said the most amazing thing. He looked out at everyone and said, "Look at me. I was so nervous about talking in front of you that at first I couldn't even get started. You may feel the same way about joining a chess club. It is not about how great you play, it's about having fun and learning whatever you can about chess. I sure hope you'll think about joining." Then he ended by saying, "Let's hear it for the Mercier Movers!"

Everyone cheered and clapped. Mrs. Starck was right; this was all about "celebrating," this time a lot of firsts. A lot!!

After the assembly, Jack, Tommy, and I hung out with our parents and Mrs. Harrington for a few minutes and then we went back to class for snack and to start our work. I could hardly think about studying, I was so excited. Tommy kept dissing me, telling me to get on task. Each time I looked up at him I couldn't stop thinking of what he had said about Jack and me today. I would never forget it.

Chapter Sixteen

The chess club was so popular that they had to hire another instructor because so many kids signed up. Tommy, Jack, and I were helpers and we went around and helped teach some of the kids who were having a lot of trouble learning how to play. I think we all looked forward to it each week and it bonded us together, kind of like the three "H's" in Boston. When I was busy, sometimes Jack and Tommy had an overnight together, but I never felt like the odd man out. It just wasn't like that with us. It just wasn't.

By April vacation, I had won so many tournaments on the weekends that I was invited to this big tournament out in Colorado in June. It's kind of expensive and I wasn't sure if I would go, but I was very excited about my rating and the fact that I had been chosen. It's called the "Kings of K–12 Chess Tournament" and Dawn was also invited to attend. This was that special tournament she had talked about when we first met, but I didn't know the name of it then or much about it. If I did well in it, Mom and Dad might be willing to pay the expenses for the National Elementary Tournament next year. I tried not to think too far ahead.

My hockey team won the state championship and they invited me to the hockey dinner and even gave me a trophy. I felt kind of funny taking it since I didn't even end up getting to many of the games, but our coach said that I was there in spirit. It seemed like so long ago since I had played hockey and it was so strange how my life ended up with chess. So strange.

The following month I had to see Dr. Roberts and have my scoliosis checked. I was learning that scoliosis wasn't the worst thing I could have since mine had stayed pretty quiet and Dr. Roberts was right: It let me do anything I wanted. Dawn was not so lucky and she would be having surgery on her back in early July. She was actually psyched about this, which seemed so odd. She said that she had worn her brace a long time and she was ready for them to fix her and get rid of the brace. I found out that her sister had scoliosis, too, but she didn't need surgery or even a brace. Dawn was kind of dissing her for that. Dawn said that she didn't think scoliosis ever went away. I guess it just stays with you kind of like freckles or maybe a birthmark. The only difference was that Dawn said sometimes you couldn't even see the scoliosis, kind of like mine.

Consuela called a lot to see how my chess was going. She was really excited about the big tournament I'd been invited to and said that even if I didn't go, the big thing was just being invited. Then one day she called and said that she had decided to stay in Georgia for the summer. That felt kind of strange, not having my sister home anymore. Mom looked really sad about it, but Grampy said that Mom did the same thing to him and Grammy. Besides, this house is never, ever empty. That's for sure.

When I was invited to the Kings of K–12, we found out that I only had to pay for my plane ticket. The tournament sponsor was going to pay for the hotel room and all my food and I was even allowed to bring a parent if they didn't mind paying for the plane ticket and food. Since my birthday is in late May, my parents decided I could go to the tournament as an early birthday present. They had to give it to me early because you had to accept the invitation to the tournament a month ahead. This was going to be the most awesome present that I had ever gotten for any birthday. I guess, if you were really into competitive chess, I had reached an amazing rating for someone who just started playing. Lots of people liked to watch me play, which in the beginning made me a little nervous. Now, I would pretend they were not even there. Dawn was the one who helped me figure out how to do this.

When the day came for me to go to Dr. Roberts, I was supposed to be taking an important test at school. I couldn't believe that I was missing the one part of the testing that I did the best in. I ended up being in a real slump all the way to the doctor's office. And then, to beat all, Dr. Roberts was running late. I was dissing this whole scene and my mom didn't look too happy either.

Finally the nurse came in and said that Dr. Roberts had just arrived and we could go into an examining room. When Dr. Roberts entered, he looked dead tired.

"Harry, these things happen and I'm sorry to be so late seeing you. I almost canceled but I knew there were no other appointments for quite some time. Thank you for being so patient."

He asked me to stand up and walk a bit with the johnny open so he could look at my back. Then he asked me to hold my arms out straight to the side and then had me bend over like I was going to dive. Dr. Roberts was often very quiet when he first started to examine me. Then he asked me to hop up on the examining table so he could check out my arms, legs, and hips.

While he examined me, he asked how the chess was coming. I couldn't believe that he remembered. I told him about my tournaments and my trip to Colorado in June.

"Harry, you certainly have done well. I bet your whole family is very proud of you. I think things with your back are going along fine, too, and I won't need to see you again for six months. The curve may have increased very slightly, but until we do another X ray, we can't be absolutely sure. For now, there is nothing to worry about."

While I was getting dressed, my mom asked Dr. Roberts a few questions about the scoliosis and then he moved on. I could tell he was in a hurry and that a lot of people were waiting for him.

On the way out, Mom set up my next appointment and was able to get a late afternoon time so I wouldn't have to miss school. In six months I would be in the middle school. Hard to believe.

It was too late to go to school so Mom and I grabbed a quick ice cream and headed for the grocery store. She had taken a vacation day so she didn't have to worry about going into the hospital. I loved going to the grocery store since I could pick out my own snacks. Most of the time I'm in school when Mom shops.

Once I made up my math test, all I could think about was my trip to Colorado and Mrs. Lamont figured that out pretty fast. At least once a day she would tell me to get back on task. I just wanted to be in Colorado, not in Massachusetts. I had never taken a trip that big in my whole life.

In early June, during our writing time, Mrs. Lamont asked each of us to write about a change that had happened in our lives. She gave lots of examples and hers was about the day she and her husband bought their first house. She wrote about how they had to stop going on nice trips and how she had to learn how to paint and wallpaper.

I had such a hard time trying to web all the changes that had happened in my life since my hockey accident. I had almost too many ideas: my hockey accident, Jack, Tommy, chess, scoliosis, Consuela staying in Atlanta, and my trip to Colorado. Mrs. Lamont convinced me that I should pick just one of these ideas and write about it.

I sat there thinking of which idea I would use. I decided that the one thing that had changed my whole life as a Boston student coming to the burbs was finally having friends willing to come and visit me where I live. This was something that I waited for and waited for and I wondered if it would ever finally happen. I love where I live and my front stoop is as important to me as any tree house in the country. They climb up a ladder and I climb up stairs. That's the only real difference.

Of all the papers I had ever written, I wrote this one the fastest and I had hardly any editing to do. I finished my first draft in three writing periods. When I showed it to Mrs. Lamont, she looked surprised that I was done so fast. Then she started reading it and I could tell she liked it just as much as I did. I ended up reading the final copy to my class a week later. This was the story that I had written in my mind many, many times. But it was finally a true one.

Chapter Seventeen

*"I'll tell you a little secret, Harry. Even though
I am always telling you to 'stand tall' and be
proud of who you are, in my eyes you have
been standin' tall since the day you were born."*

It was hard to believe that I would be getting on an airplane
with my dad and my Grampy to go to the Kings of K–12
Chess Tournament in Colorado. I had never been on an airplane before and neither had my Grampy. I thought he was
even more excited than I was. Mom said that Grampy had
been packed for three weeks!

I was kind of sad that Jeb wasn't on the bus, but I think he
was probably tired of me talking about chess. I couldn't
believe he didn't diss me sometimes for that. I was hoping that
my bus wouldn't be late so I could have some time with Jack
before class. I sure wished he could go to Colorado with me.

He and his dad had come to more than half of my local tournaments, which was really amazing. Jack and I had become like brothers.

As I was getting off the bus, I asked Mr. Barrett for the time. "We're early for once," I thought to myself. "I should be able to catch Jack in the cafeteria."

I rushed off the bus, but when I got into the cafeteria no one in my class was there. I was so disappointed. Jack was the one person who really understood how excited I was about going to Colorado to play in the tournament and I couldn't even have cafeteria time with him before class. Just when my bus was early, there was no one around to see it. As I walked down the hall to class, everything seemed more quiet than usual. My classroom door was already shut.

Miss Hatzis from across the hall peered over and said, "You can go right in, Harry. Someone must have closed the door by mistake."

As I opened the door, Tommy jumped out in front of me and everyone yelled "Surprise!" In the back of the room, the kids were holding up a banner that said, "Good luck, Harry. You are always a winner to us." My whole class had signed it. My mom was standing over in the corner of the room with my Grampy. Mrs. Starck and Mrs. Lamont were off to the other side. Mom and Grampy had watery eyes. Right next to my mom were Jeb, Herbie, and Hank. I couldn't believe it! Jack was standing next to them with this big grin on his face.

Herbie yelled out, "Whassssssup chess king," and everyone started to laugh.

There were all kinds of things to eat: coffee cakes, donuts, muffins, and juice and milk to drink. Mrs. Lamont let the kids ask me any questions they wanted about chess and how I got interested in it. My Grampy looked so proud when I told them how he and I played. I told them about my dad and me, too. I knew if my dad could have been there, he would have been so proud. I had wondered why my dad kept telling me what a busy day he was having at work. He must have been trying to let me know ahead of time why he couldn't be at this party. Now it all fit.

After I finished answering all the questions and the party was winding down, my principal asked me if I wanted to give

Chapter Seventeen

Jeb, Hank, and Herbie a tour of the school. Jeb passed because he had to get over to his own school, but Hank and Herbie were all excited. My Grampy even decided to come. While Mom drove Jeb over to his school, I gave the tour to Grampy and the "brothers." Mrs. Starck came along to the first few classes and talked to my Grampy while I hung out with Herbie and Hank. I could hear Grampy giving Mrs. Starck an earful about how school had changed from when he was young. He remembered so many things about his time there. Some of the things he was telling her I never knew and even Hank and Herbie started listening. When Grampy told my principal that he had to really "stand tall" when he was in school, it made me smile to myself.

"School may be better today," Grampy went on to say, "except the one thing that you don't find in all these fancy books and fast-moving things like the computer is that these young people need to feel proud of who they are. Nobody is teaching them how to stand tall and that's what this life is all about. It doesn't matter how much money you have or how smart you are, or who you read about, the young people always need to remember to 'stand tall' and be proud of who they are."

Mrs. Starck stopped for a minute at the bottom of the stairs leading up to the next floor. She looked over at Grampy and then me and this big warm smile came on her face.

"You know, Harry. Your Grampy is a very wise man, and I think there's a lot of your Grampy inside you. We're lucky to have you as part of our school family."

Then she put out her hand to my Grampy, told him how much she had enjoyed meeting him, and said good-bye.

I had such a special feeling inside me that I couldn't even put it into words. I knew my Grampy felt it, too. I could tell just by the way he looked at me.

Then Herbie broke the quiet by saying, "What does she mean by school family? I mean, check us out. We sure don't look like we all came from the same place."

Hank started dissing Herbie, and Grampy and I started laughing. Nobody would ever change Herbie.

After I showed everyone the rest of my school, we went back downstairs to my classroom. My mom was waiting for us and scooped up Grampy and Hank and Herbie to drive them back to Boston. My Grampy looked like he wanted to stay for the rest of the day and I could tell my mom was on to this.

"Come on, Dad, time to go. You already did fourth grade a long time ago."

Grampy looked over at my class and said, "Guess I have to go now. I'm not allowed to do fourth grade again."

Everyone started to laugh. Then Tommy called out, "Good-bye, Grampy." And the rest of the class did the same. I just wished my dad and Consuela could have been there. Then it would have been a perfect day, but I still thought it was my best one ever in school.

I spent the rest of the day trying hard not to think of my plane trip and the tournament, but it was hard not to think about it all. Each time I looked up I'd see Jack or even Tommy with this twinkle in their eyes and I knew they were as excited as I was.

At about two o'clock Mrs. Lamont told us to pack up our backpacks. I kept thinking to myself that she couldn't tell time. But just as I was finishing up, I looked up and there was my dad standing in the doorway. Mrs. Lamont introduced him to the kids and some of them remembered him from the school assembly announcing the chess club.

"Harry has to leave us a little early today, class, so I thought we could take a few minutes to wish him luck," said Mrs. Lamont.

I answered a few more questions and then each of my classmates gave me a card they had made. I couldn't wait to read them all. I never had a day this special in my whole life. I never, ever felt so good.

On the way home in the car, Dad and I talked about the morning surprise and how Grampy gave his "stand tall" talk to my principal. I was so glad my dad picked me up. He told me how sorry he was about his big meeting in the morning.

"The problem is, Harry, that your school is kind of far away from where I work, so there is no way to just go to a meeting at work and then rush out and catch your school event. I am really sorry I missed it all, son."

Ever since I started in the program, I knew that the distance to school could be hard sometimes. As Grampy says, "You can't change the map!"

On the way home I started to doze off a little. I kept thinking about my day. It was so sweet. And I knew that for my whole life I would always remember Mrs. Lamont for doing this for me. She was the fairest and hardest teacher I had ever had and she had this special thing about her that had really helped me connect to my school and to my class. I couldn't explain it, but it made me feel so good when I was around her. She just seemed to look at me and know what I was feeling.

When I got home there seemed to be a lot of rushing around in my house. The doorbell rang and rang and once a man arrived from the newspaper and asked if he could get a picture of me with my chessboard. I knew that I had won a lot of tournaments in a much shorter time than most chess players my age, because some of the chess people had told my dad that I was a "late-comer" to the tournament scene and a "chess wonder." When my dad and I began to talk to the newspaper man, I started to get this funny feeling that this might jinx my game. Grampy, who was sitting next to me, told me not to worry, that they did this stuff a lot for famous young people. When the reporter heard Grampy say that, he looked up and gave Grampy one of those smiles that goes between my parents sometimes, kind of like they are speakin' a special language or something.

After dinner I went to my room and sat on my bed reading all the cards that my classmates had made for me. I had never gotten so many cards in my life and each one made me feel so happy inside. Jack, who does this awesome cartoon stuff, made a little card with all these cartoon boxes of me playing in the tournament. And then in the last box I was standing up a winner. The only thing you could see in the box was me standing and all these hands in the background with little balloons calling me awesome, a rocker, amazing. Jack even tried to throw in some of what we call "Herbie specials," and it looked so funny in a card from someone who is not African-American because Jack didn't know exactly how to use the comments. I began laughing so hard I could feel the tears in my eyes. This card was definitely a keeper, even if I didn't win.

Tommy's card had all these arrows pointing to different ideas and then on the very back he had one last arrow and next to it he wrote, "No one has even been as nice to me as you."

I sat on my bed and looked at his card for a long time, thinking. In third grade Tommy and I were friends, but this year he did that mean snack thing at the beginning of the year and now he was nicer than ever. I hoped he could stay this way.

Consuela called to wish me luck and after I hung up the phone, I felt sad that she couldn't be there at the tournament. Then I started to feel really, really sad about my mom not going. My mom doesn't like flying and so my Grampy would be coming with us. My mom said her stomach gets weird when she flies and my dad said it gets worse than weird.

Mom and Dad came in and said good night to me and asked me how I was feeling about all this special stuff. I was starting to get this strange feeling in my tummy and so I told them about it. My dad said he got that feeling, too. He said it's a little nerves, a lot of excitement, and then all this other stuff that he went on and on about. Finally, my mom put him on "stop" and they said good night.

Grampy wandered in next. I knew he had been waiting for Mom and Dad to finish.

"Harry, I want you to pretend your bed is the front stoop, okay?"

"No problem, Grampy," I answered.

"You know, Harry. I never had a son, and after your mother was born we went through some hard times and I guess the dear Lord thought that one child was plenty for your Grammy and Grampy. When your mama brought your daddy home, I felt pretty happy. But I knew that he belonged to your mama and I didn't want to hog him all the time asking him to do stuff. That would have made big trouble with your mama because he needed to be takin' care of her. Having Consuela come into this family with your daddy was something very special. Very special, indeed. And then, Harry, when you were born, son, I knew that the dear Lord was still watching over me. I'll tell you a little secret, Harry. Even though I am always telling you to 'stand tall' and be proud of who you are, in my eyes you have been standin' tall since the day you were born. No matter what happens in this big-deal tournament, just remember, Harry, what an honor it is that you got this far. I think you already know you're a winner, Harry. On the day of that tournament, when you sit down at that chessboard, I think you're going to feel taller than you ever have in your whole life. I just know you'll have that feeling inside you. And I know that people are gonna be looking at you, including your Great-Grampy from heaven. He's the man who taught me how to 'stand tall' and be proud of who I am."

I looked at my Grampy and I was about to give him this big hug when he put out his hand to me and said, "Famous people shake hands, Harry."

We both got into laughin' so hard. As he was walking out of my bedroom, I called out to him, "Grampy, you're taller than the Prudential Tower."

He looked back at me with this big smile that was as good as the hug I didn't get.

Chapter Eighteen

Getting up early in the morning is not so bad if you know you are going to do something really special. Mom was driving us all to the airport.

As soon as we got to the part of the airport where we had to wait for the plane, I spotted Dawn. When she saw me, she started waving and my parents went over and began talking to her mom and dad. Dawn and I were both invited to the tournament. We had become chess friends and I looked forward to seeing her at tournaments. Dawn's brace didn't stop her from doing anything. She even joked about how her new opponents were distracted by the brace, so she sometimes got a move up on them. I always updated her on my back and it was another kind of connection we had besides chess.

While we waited for the plane, Dawn and I rapped about chess and chess ratings and all the stuff that you have to know when you play tournament chess. She had been doing this since she was eight so she had been in lots of chess tournaments. I was so impressed with how much she knew. She was really awesome.

The plane ride seemed to go on forever. We had to make one stop halfway to Colorado. Each time we took off or landed, my Grampy squeezed my hand so hard that I started to wonder if I'd be able to use it in the tournament. Finally, my dad looked over and told Grampy to go easy on my hands. But Grampy still didn't let go. When the plane finally landed at the Denver airport, everyone clapped. Grampy put his two fingers in his mouth and gave out a whistle that made everyone around us roar with laughter. We weren't even out of the plane and already he had a fan club.

We were staying right in the hotel where the tournament would take place. I had never seen anything like it in my whole life. Everyone was making me feel like I was some kind of special person. The place even had an indoor swimming pool that Dad said we could go in as soon as we unpacked and got settled. He wanted to let the organizers know I had arrived so that I would be paired in the first round. After all, that was why we were there.

After we did all that stuff, Dad and I put on our swimsuits and T-shirts and headed for the pool. Grampy said he would stay in the room and wait for a phone call. I thought that was kind of different, but Grampy is not a swimmer so maybe he just used that as a reason for not going.

When we got to the pool, I heard a very loud voice and it was Dawn, who was over in the deep end with her mom and dad. It was the first time I'd seen her without her brace. She was about to go off the diving board. I headed down in her direction with my dad following behind me.

While Dawn and I enjoyed the pool and she introduced me to some of the other kids in the tournament, all the parents chatted. When it came time to get out of the pool, my dad really hadn't had more than a five-minute "dip" as he calls it. Talk, talk, talk. That's a parent thing, I guess.

After the swim, we headed for our room to see how Grampy was doing. As we were coming in, he looked over at my dad with this mischievous look on his face and said, "Got the call. We're all set, H. P. Junior."

My dad just nodded and walked away. I was kind of wondering what this was all about, but nobody was talking.

After we changed, we headed downstairs to this amazing room where they were having a reception for all the chess players and their families. All the players got free T-shirts with the words "Kings of K–12 Chess Tournament" written across the front. Then on the back of the shirt was my name, which was so awesome and made me feel like someone really special. Then they had all this other stuff for us: pencils with the name of the tournament on them, programs with a scoresheet for each game of the tournament, water bottles, and even a backpack to put it all in with one of the sponsors' names on it. I felt like it was Christmas or something.

Chapter Eighteen

Grampy kept following me around and each time he saw a new souvenir, he said, "Oh, Lordy, will you look at this!" Everybody already knew he was Grampy and each time I looked up he had someone else with him.

Talking to the other players and meeting their families was something special. I was a little sad that Mom and Consuela couldn't be there, but I knew it cost a lot of money to come so far. Besides, as Mom said, I would remember Grampy coming to this with my dad and me for the rest of my life.

Dawn kind of adopted me and while we were walking around, she made sure I met everyone there and she told them how good I was at chess and the very short time I'd been playing in tournaments.

Dinner was provided by the organizers. They had this buffet with every kind of food imaginable. Some of the stuff I had never eaten before, but it sure was good. And the desserts. Whoa, baby. What a choice. If I'd tasted all of them, I'd be rolling into that tournament for sure.

At about eight-thirty we began saying good night and heading upstairs. I was on such a high that I couldn't believe this was all happening to me. It was like a dream. I'd never be able to sleep. You know what that meant, no sleep, no dreams!

Our room faced the mountains and after Dad and Grampy went to sleep, I got out of bed and just looked out at the full moon and the shadows the mountains made against it. I stood there thinking about Grampy and my mind went back to the day when he had told me about my Great-Grampy. I started thinking about how my Great-Grampy had to make his own chess pieces and hide them so no one would break them. And then I thought about Grampy and how kind he was and how much he had helped me to really care about even the people who were not nice to me. I looked up at the mountains and the moon and I whispered quietly to myself, "This tournament is for you Great-Grampy and I hope you'll be watching me."

I climbed back into bed and for a minute I thought my Grampy was awake. I really wanted to say something to him. I quickly looked again, but when I heard his snoring I knew that he was still asleep.

The next morning we were up very early even though the first round was not until eleven o'clock. My dad told Grampy and me to eat breakfast without him because he had some special thing to do. I was kind of surprised that he'd miss breakfast and he was acting so jumpy, but I was happy to eat with Grampy.

While we were sitting there having breakfast in the same fancy room where we had eaten dinner, my Grampy kept staring at me. Finally, I said, "Grampy, you have this huge smile on your face and you're not even eating this good food."

My Grampy was quiet for a minute and then his eyes got all watery, kind of like my mom's.

"This is one of the proudest moments of my whole, entire life, Harry," he said. "It doesn't even matter if you win or lose. What's important is that here you are standing so tall, Harry Jones, standing so tall."

At first I wanted to answer him, but I didn't know how. I just sat there looking at Grampy and watched him squeezing my hands, looking at me with those big, brown, proud eyes.

After breakfast Grampy and I wandered around the hotel gift shop. From the gift shop we went into the skittles room and played some bughouse chess as teammates. Bughouse is a form of chess in which two teams play each other. There are two people on each team. When a player captures an opponent's piece on his board, he gives it to his partner. The partner can place the man on his own board instead of making a move. Playing with Grampy kind of relaxed me before my tournament rounds.

Dad finally joined us a little before eleven, when my first round was starting. He looked at Grampy with this big silly grin on his face and Grampy just nodded back. I didn't think much of it because I was busy looking at all the sensory boards in the room that allowed the friends of the chess players to watch the tournament from their hometowns. It was pretty exciting how they had a computer hooked up to every board.

In the program, they had what they called a feature article about each one of us. I could tell that Dad and Grampy were trying to get as many extra programs as they could.

Chapter Eighteen

"This booklet will probably go out to every relative we have," I thought to myself.

When it was time for everybody to sit down and begin, I looked over at Dawn and smiled. The room was very quiet and I was very nervous. All you could see were long tables with chessboards and black and white chess pieces. The computer flipped a coin. It gave Dawn and all the odd-numbered players in the top half of our section white. White had a little advantage since it always got the first move. Dawn happened to be the highest-rated player in the tournament.

I would be playing with the black pieces. I had two hours to make forty moves and if neither flag had fallen before black finished his fortieth move, then we would go to sudden death, which gave each of us another hour in addition to any time we had left over from the first time control. If I won the first five rounds, I would be playing for the championship in the final round.

The days had been long. Four days of high-caliber tournament chess had me worn out and I still had today and tomorrow to go. By the end of the day the mountains in the background were being reflected by a beautiful full moon. Dawn looked as tired as I did and both of us had won each of our rounds, leaving us only this round and one other to determine who would be playing in the final round. It was clear that Dawn and I might be competing against each other, although neither of us said anything about it.

My opponent for the fifth round was a boy from Mexico who spoke very little English. He had this wonderful smile that looked as if it was permanently fixed on his face. I was feeling so nervous that I couldn't even think about smiling. The round seemed long. My opponent was very good. The only other people in our section still playing were Dawn and her opponent. I quickly looked away and noticed that Dawn's opponent was moving his chair. Their game seemed to have ended. I had a really good position. My opponent only had one defense, but he didn't see it. He played a different move and then, six moves later, I checkmated him. I had won the semifinal round.

I quietly got up and left the area that still had other players in their own age-group tournament. In each corner of this very large room there must have been about ten tournaments going on.

I was escorted out of the room and went down the hallway into a room where families could sit and watch a computer monitor.

From out of nowhere came this "Harry! You won! You won!"

I followed the voice with my eyes. Way in the back of this room, almost hiding, I could see Jack, my mom, and Consuela standing next to my Grampy and Dad. My parents and my sister and even my Grampy had tears in their eyes and kind of looked like they were each holding back a flood.

"I couldn't believe that they were all there," I thought to myself. "Especially Consuela and Jack."

So that's why my dad and Grampy were actin' so weird. I looked at the wall charts with the scores and saw that Dawn and I would be playing for the championship of our age group in the sixth and final round. Who would ever have thought that we would be opponents in the final round of such an important tournament? I glanced over at Dawn and I knew she was thinking the same thing.

We both smiled and as I stood there, I got a feeling in my body like something I had never experienced before. Almost a rush! Then I knew what it was all about. Grampy was so right. It didn't really matter whether Dawn won or I won, because standing there in Denver, Colorado, I felt taller than those mountains out there and proud of who I was: Harry Jones, a finalist in the Kings K–12 Chess Tournament.

"Great-Grampy, this tournament is for you. Hope you're watching."

Epilogue

You'll have to wait to see if Harry or Dawn wins the final round of the tournament. The same is going to be true of Harry's scoliosis. You'll just have to wait and see if and how it progresses. Harry will continue to see Dr. Roberts, perhaps every six months or only every three months, depending on the progression of Harry's curve. What's important is that just as Harry adjusted to his hockey injury, the same is true of his scoliosis. There are boys all over the country just like Harry who are followed by orthopedic surgeons regularly with the hope that by the time they reach full growth, their scoliosis will still be at a manageable stage.

However, as is true of many medical conditions, there are varying degrees. Dawn clearly is experiencing a more serious progression to her curve and although the bracing has helped her scoliosis, her curve is such that surgery is now necessary.

I hope you enjoyed meeting Harry. If you're one of those children who is bused every day from your city to another community for school, I'm sure you have appreciated reading about Harry's journey. And especially for those of you who stay in the same community for school, perhaps you have learned to open your mind and your heart to the journey that other students travel, and not just in distance. Remember, to be a good friend it is important to appreciate the life each of you lives. I hope each and every one of you will always "stand tall and be proud of who you are."

About The Author

Mary Mahony is an elementary-school resource teacher and strong advocate for multiculturalism. She has spent many years working with families whose children are embarked on a variety of journeys — educational, social, and medical. Mary is the mother of three children: Breen, an architect; Colin, who is currently completing a master's in business administration; and Erin, who is a first-year medical student. Mary's first book, *What Can I Give You*, chronicles her daughter's journey with congenital scoliosis. Her second book, *There's an 'S' on My Back*, focuses on the adventures of Maisey MacGuire, a fifth grader diagnosed with scoliosis at a school screening.

Mary makes use of her own experiences to understand children and the challenges they face. She reminds us that "if we are good listeners, sometimes children can be our teachers."